The Lands

K. Newman

The Lands

Copyright © 2014 K. Newman

Rivershore Books

ACKNOWLEDGEMENTS

A special thank you to my husband, Chad, for encouraging my dreams. My parents, John and Michelle Huffman, for always believing in me and supporting me. My brother, Steve Huffman, for putting visual art to my dreams. And finally, my sister, Trisha Huffman, for being understanding.

Loved and Inspired

Front cover photo and design by: Steven J. Huffman of Bright Light Photography

Prologue

Teagan watched in horror as the following events played out in slow motion; Her older sister's eyes caught on something and lit up in delight. Teagan had a feeling, and ran towards her, yelling "Nooooo!!!" but it was too late. Jessa put her hands on the ledge of the ship, and without looking back or hesitating, she jumped. Teagan reached the side of the ship just as her sister plunged deep into the most beautiful expanse of glittering, blue water. Several others did as Jessa did, but Teagan's eyes were transfixed on the activity below.

A mass of boulders jutted out of the water. Other people were lying on those smooth rocks, and they appeared to be enjoying the sun. Hundreds of people were laughing and splashing around in the great big water. Teagan's eyes grew wide as she saw there were more than just people in the water—there were huge fish and killer whales! Teagan yelled at Jessa to watch out; a big fish was coming her way. Tears were beginning to flow from her eyes as she watched her sister swim towards the boulders. Jessa seemed to be in a trance and was going to the boulders for a specific reason.

Micah came up behind Teagan and pulled her into his arms, letting her cry. She felt she had lost her older sister to something they couldn't explain. She was still alive, just no longer with them.

"What is going on, Micah?" Teagan asked her older brother.

"None of this makes sense. I don't know what is going on," Micah answered, trying to be calm by breathing slowly, it did not seem to be working. He only hoped Teagan would not notice.

Teagan couldn't believe that for the first time her older brother, who always had answers, couldn't explain the situation.

She looked up at him with fresh tears. "We have to get her back. How are we going to get her back?"

"I don't think we can, but we will find more answers. We have to," Micah answered.

"What if I lose you, too? What if I watch my family get taken away from me, one by one?" Teagan couldn't stop sobbing.

Chapter 1

"I don't understand why we are going to visit them after so many years. What does it matter anymore?" Jessa whined.

"Well, I miss them, sweetheart, and they have been trying to get us to visit for a long time now and the whole family finally has time." Jessa's mother, Malorey, replied.

"I don't miss them, so why do I have to go? Heck, why does the whole family have to go?" Jessa asked.

"Janessa Avery Robinson, I don't understand why it is such a big deal that the family goes on a short vacation to meet up with some old family friends." Malorey was starting to sound displeased.

"Hey—I'm with Jessa. I don't see why we all have to go." Teagan added.

"See! How about Teagan and I just hang out here, in Minnesota, for the week while you, Dad, and Micah go?" Jessa tried to compromise.

"Nope; the Thornbergs made it very clear that the whole family had to come. They are extremely excited and have a lot of things they want to show us. They also mentioned to pack for all kinds of weather just in case, so make sure to pack layers and a swimsuit." Malorey said.

"It appears we have lost this battle, Teagan," Jessa said quietly.

Teagan responded, "As a matter of fact I *did* want to go on a boring, pointless trip!"

"Well, we can't blame the Thornbergs for their persistence. Every year around this same time they invite us to visit. Fortunately we have had an excuse not to go every year," Jessa said as she marched up to the room she'd grown up in and began to pack.

"Except until now, apparently." Teagan said just before she blasted music and texted some friends to cancel the plans she had made with them.

Teagan refused to pack out of frustration and confusion. Micah wasn't there yet anyway, she reasoned, so there was no rush. Teagan couldn't keep from smiling at the thought of how Micah was going to react to the news. Just as this entered her mind, she heard the front door shut and the echo of Micah's voice flowed up the stairs.

Micah was their last hope. Teagan met Jessa in the hallway as they listened to their parents tell Micah the plan. They didn't hear any yelling or loud voices. Teagan looked at Jessa questioningly; Jessa just shrugged in response. Soon they saw Micah come up the stairs with his luggage.

He cocked his head to the side. "I thought for sure you two would have outgrown the whole 'eavesdropping' habit you have."

The two young ladies squealed and ran to Micah to give him hugs; it had been a long time since they had seen him. The holidays were the only time the whole family got together, since they were in grade school. They followed him to his old room and sat down on the bed as he set his luggage on one of the dressers.

"So? Did you talk them out of it?" Teagan asked.

"Talk them out of what?" Micah turned to the two ladies, who had expectant looks on their faces.

"Out of the trip, Micah!" Jessa said before Teagan

could answer.

"Well, I'm not exactly excited about the idea, but there will be beaches and hot chicks, so it's hard to argue that." Micah shrugged.

"I'm constantly in warm weather. I go to college in California, just in case you forgot," Jessa answered.

Teagan cut in, feeling like they were losing focus on the issue. "Are you joking? You aren't even friends with the Thornbergs, Micah!"

"Hey, I tried to tell them it would be nice to just stay here, since we are only here around holidays and it's nice to be back at home every once in a while. The snow and the holidays do go together, but one thing I have learned over the years is when Mom gets that look in her eyes there is no hope of changing her mind," Micah answered calmly.

They looked at him with a measure of disgust. Micah sighed. "Look, let's just make the best of the time we all have together. I imagine this will be the last time it will be just us."

"What is that supposed to mean?" Jessa asked.

"It means we are getting older and things might come up—or one of us might bring an outsider to the family gatherings…you know, a boyfriend or girlfriend. As it is, I had a tough time getting out of work for this week. Besides, I don't go to college in California, like someone—if you've forgotten, I live in New York, and the weather is cold there too, so having a trip south to visit the Thornbergs doesn't sound that bad." Micah responded.

"What, so you have a girlfriend?" Teagan asked.

"No, but I wasn't just talking about me." Micah chuckled.

Jessa rolled her eyes. "This is ridiculous." She left to continue packing. Teagan followed.

The airplane ride was a short one, but just enough for the Jessa, Teagan, and Micah to get into a fight or two. The Thornbergs' directions were a little questionable. They were told not to get a rental, but the Thornbergs were not able to pick them up; they had insisted they take a shuttle bus. The address led to what was called 'The Depot'; Mrs. Robinson wasn't the first one to comment on the strangeness of the address given and had contacted Mrs. Thornberg to double check the instructions given.

"I swear that family has gotten stranger over the years. I thought they just wanted us to visit really badly, but their excitement is making me a little uncomfortable," Mrs. Robinson said.

"Really? You wait until we're here to finally agree that this was a stupid idea!" Jessa yelled as they got out of the shuttle bus and walked into The Depot.

"Well, it is a bit odd that we couldn't just go to their house. What do you think, Jack?" Malorey was starting to look even more concerned as she took in the view at The Depot; it was unlike anything she had seen.

"Well, sweetheart, we came all the way down here, so we may as well make the most of it," Jack responded.

"Mom?" Micah asked, bewildered.

All five members of the family stood inside the building, and all five lacked the ability to find words; what they were seeing was beyond anything they could comprehend. What they were seeing did not make sense. They were miles from any large water source, but The Depot had a large ship stationed like a train, loading people one-by-one, as if it were an everyday occurrence to see a large ship, with large masts and sails, floating on nothing but what appeared to be air. It was a magnificent ship, and the size was not missed on any of the Robinsons. It was a ship out of a time that had long passed. The massive ship had only one way in or out of The Depot. Jack followed the direction that seemed to be the only way out; it was a tube-like structure that led upwards instead of straight out—almost like it led to the sky.

"This is impossible," Jack whispered to Malorey.

"Are we hallucinating?" Malorey asked in response.

"Mom, what did you put in those fruit snacks that you gave us on the plane?" Micah exclaimed.

"First of all, nothing. Second, it is surprising that a 24 year old still needs mommy to pack snacks at all. All three of you kids are over the age of 18. Don't blame me," Malorey responded sarcastically as the Robinsons continued to take in what was going on around them.

There was not a ticket booth to purchase tickets for a voyage—which begged the question as to how one was to gain passage on the vessel. The Depot looked like something out of the days when trains were the best mode of transportation for long distances. The ushers and staff were dressed as if they lived in that time period as well.

Jessa started moving towards the loading area before the rest of the Robinson family followed. Teagan thought it was odd that they were unloading luggage from the ship rather than loading it. She watched closely just to make sure it wasn't being moved to a different spot on the ship. She saw it brought to a large container that seemed to organize the luggage nicely. Teagan gripped her luggage more tightly, shaking her head.

"Maybe they just want to go for a quick, unusual boat ride to start out?" Malorey reasoned as they continued to walk towards the loading plank.

"With what tickets, Mom?" Jessa asked.

"Let's just go up and talk to the man with the clipboard; maybe he has further instructions, or can point us in the right direction," Malorey responded. The Robinson family cautiously walked in that direction. There was a bustle of people walking in all directions, and on more than one occasion the Robinsons had to dodge out of the way of a staff member or an eager tourist.

The man with the clipboard greeted the Robinson family with a warm smile, introduced himself as Sam, and asked for their names. Malorey gave their last name and then proceeded to introduce the rest of the family. She tried to say they didn't know what was going on, but Sam interrupted her by calling for a petite woman.

"Anita, please take this family to the best spot on the ship; the Thornbergs requested this for them. Also, please inform the Thornbergs of their arrival," Sam instructed as he handed her five long pieces of rope.

Anita curtsied to the Robinson family and gently asked them to follow her. People were being seated throughout the top deck of the ship, the front of the boat was completely full, and the middle section was quickly showing the same. The Robinson family, however, was shown to the very back of the ship and told where to sit. In complete bewilderment, each family member filed into their row and took their seat. There wasn't anyone seated in front of them yet, so Anita took that opportunity to stand in front of them and give some instructions. First she handed each of them a rope about five feet in length.

"So the back of the ship is considered the best spot. I beg to differ," Teagan whispered to Jessa, who smiled back at her. They both recalled the days of waiting in line for a roller coaster, and always having to wait longer for the front.

"You are considered the VIP of this voyage. The Thornbergs are highly respected and wanted you to be treated thus. They will be joining you shortly after I go over a few things of importance. First, always, *always* keep that rope with you. Even if you leave the ship, keep it with you. It has now become the most important of your possessions. I have seen individuals tie it around their waist like a belt to make sure they don't forget it. You may want to do this."

"What do you mean, 'leave the ship'?" Teagan questioned.

Anita smiled in response but did not answer as she continued to explain. Jessa couldn't believe how interesting her accent was; she sounded like she went through a special prep school to speak so properly. The only thing Jessa actually heard was to keep the rope with her at all times, so she tied it around her waist—against her better fashion judgment. Teagan reluctantly followed and Micah did the same.

"You don't have to stay in your seats. As soon as we are on our way, you are free to move around the deck. Food will be served throughout your time on the ship if you become hungry." She smiled and then continued, "The Thornbergs are here now." She excused herself.

The Thornbergs greeted them with big smiles and hugs. Mrs. Thornberg could not be more ecstatic, and talked so fast that the Robinsons were having trouble following the conversation.

Malorey cut in after a short while. "We missed you too; it seemed that we heard from you about once a year, always wanting us to visit. I had no idea you had booked a fun trip like this for us to enjoy together."

"Fun indeed—you have no idea what you are going to see!" Mrs. Thornberg said as they finally took the seats in front of them.

Mrs. Thornberg was a plump woman with dark, blonde hair that went to her shoulders. Her face was round and her features well proportioned, she looked excited at the Robinsons arrival. Mr. Thornberg was tall and imposing; although he had been smiling the entire time he still was able to have a stern look about his face.

"Where is the rest of the Thornberg crew?" Jack asked.

Mrs. Thornberg turned around in her seat. "They were not able to meet at this time, but we can always get together later—after everything is settled."

Malorey didn't miss a beat. "Everything settled? What do you mean?"

"Don't' worry, dear; you will see," Mrs. Thornberg answered cryptically

Chapter 2

When she turned around, the entire Robinson family rolled their eyes at Mrs. Thornberg's statement. It didn't take long for the ship to be completely full. Anita came around one more time to make sure everyone was comfortable and accounted for.

Jessa didn't need to mind read to know Teagan was just as skeptical of this trip. She was convinced it was a Six Flags theme park ride that used a different part of the imagination. Jessa decided she would be happy when it was over and she could lay out by the ocean. The sooner the ship left, the quicker she could do just that.

The ship made no sound, but slightly jerked forward,

which was the only indication they were moving, besides seeing The Depot move behind them. The sails puffed out beautifully, even when there was not a breeze to move them. Every member of the Robinson family gripped the arms of their chairs. The tunnel was getting closer, and Jack was pleased, knowing he predicted at least one thing on this trip so far. The family felt like they were being taken on a big roller coaster ride, but didn't know what the outcome would be.

"Well, we can't be going upside down on this roller coaster, otherwise we would have seatbelts and harnesses," Teagan said with an uneasy smile.

"We must not be going entirely too fast on this, either, or we would at the very least have seatbelts," Jessa added, trying her best not to sound nervous.

Jessa felt her heart jump and she gripped Teagan's hand; she felt the pressure given back in equal measure. *So much for not being nervous.* Jessa thought. Micah looked around for someone to jump out and say they were on some television program for practical jokes. Mr. and Mrs. Robinson were pale, as the ship continued to move forward.

The ship made its ascent through the tunnel. It opened up to a vast amount of blue sky that seemed to stretch on forever. People were beginning to get out of their seats to look at the beauty before them. Birds were gracefully flying alongside the ship. There was a warm breeze that toyed with everyone's hair and snapped the sails back tighter.

As the family looked out, they realized that at first they were floating forward, above moving cars and people walking on the streets going about their business. Jessa thought it was odd no one was looking up and pointing at the very strange sight it must have been. As they continued to watch, the city seemed to disappear, as if a thick fog settled over the entire expanse.

Mrs. Robinson had nearly become sick in the stop and go traffic of the shuttle ride to The Depot, but this ride was different. It was smooth and dreamlike. Nothing was making sense. Malorey struggled with the idea that she may have unknowingly put her family in danger. Normally, she did not make decisions without more information and a basic understanding of what was going on.

Teagan took out her cell phone to take some pictures. The phone wouldn't turn on.

"Sick, my phone died; can you take some pictures with your phone for me, Jessa?" Teagan asked.

"Sure," Jessa said as she reached in her handbag.

Both girls watched as the phone also refused to respond to the power button. The Thornbergs told the family that their electronics would not work during the trip. Jessa and looked at her wristwatch; even that had stopped working. Teagan groaned as she realized how bored she would be for the rest of the trip.

Jessa stared, dumbfounded, at Mrs. Thornberg—the one that delivered the news. Micah sighed heavily, let his head fall back, and just looked at the sky. He wished he would've tried a little harder to stay back in Minnesota.

After what seemed to be a few hours, food was passed around by ushers. Anita had checked on the Robinsons more than once to see if they needed anything. It didn't take long for them to forget about the lack of electronics. They were in complete awe of the splendor before their eyes; they had also forgotten about their appetites.

The captain came over the intercom, welcomed everyone to the ship, and informed the patrons of the first destination: Forest Land. The Robinsons looked at each other, thinking it was the oddest name for a city. The ship was coming upon a ravine with water rushing several yards below them and moss-covered cliffs on both sides of them. A few times, the cliffs were close enough to touch. It seemed as if the land itself was floating on air, bouncing up and down ever so slowly—as if nothing was holding it in place. Even though what they could see below was clearly land and a rushing river, not once did the ship actually touch the water. The further they went in through the ravine, the darker it got, with towering trees on either side. The smell of nature surrounded them as they continued to look around. The breeze became chilly and thick with moisture.

Confusion and discomfort had grown the further this trip went along. They looked to other patrons to see if they understood what was going on. Many of them were out of their seats already, they did not look as if they knew any better than the Robinsons.

"It even smells real," Malorey commented.

"It *is* real, Malorey." Mrs. Thornberg laughed.

"That's impossible—this whole thing is impossible. We aren't even floating on water, yet we are on a ship made for water," Malorey responded.

"You will get used to it, until you find a place you want to be," Mrs. Thornberg said, again, cryptically.

"What do you mean 'find a place you want to be'?" Malorey asked, but she was interrupted by someone yelling out: "Watch out!"

Everyone saw as the ship nearly hit a side of a cliff

wall. Just below them there were tree trunks that had fallen across the ravine. It looked as if the fallen trees had served as a bridge for small critters. The ship floated above the fallen tree trunks gracefully.

"What the heck is the captain doing up there? Is he drunk or something?" Jessa yelled after almost getting hit by hanging vines.

It was clear there was frustration from the other passengers at how close they came to getting hit. Just as she finished with her question, a bigger chunk of fallen trees were in view and the ship was heading right for them, giving just enough clearance between the bottom of the boat and the trees. What happened next, no one would have anticipated. Jessa, Teagan, and Micah saw about two dozen men and women jump off the side of the ship and land on the toppled trees, then they ran of into the dense forest.

"Hey, is that part of this ride?" Micah asked.

"Only if you feel like it," Anita said, behind him. He didn't even know she was there until he heard her voice.

"Holy crap; we have been drugged," Teagan whispered to her older brother and sister.

"Yeah, there is no other explanation," Jessa said as she turned to Anita and asked, "So are we going to dock here and wait for them to finish what they are doing and get back on? I mean, are there souvenirs or something up there?"

"No. We will continue on. They all have their ropes," Anita said and walked away.

"What the..." Jessa wanted to finish her question, but found it pointless.

"Where did Mom and Dad go?" Teagan asked with a tinge of fear laced in her voice.

After a moment of looking around, Micah answered, "They are over by the side of the ship with the Thornbergs."

"I'm staying right here if it is all the same to you," Jessa said firmly.

"Me too," Teagan chimed in.

"Yeah, I see no need to move," Micah added.

More trays of food were passed along, and the three of them became skeptical of the kind of food they were serving. There must be some type of hallucinogen in them. Teagan was still gripping her luggage, and then she realized that the people that jumped onto the fallen tree logs had left their luggage. *Not me,* she thought to herself.

It seemed like a few more hours had passed, even though the sun did not appear to move in the sky. Since Jessa's watch seemed to have run out of battery, she was unable to check exactly how late it was. There was a nice breeze, and the sun seemed to set the perfect temperature. Jessa got a little chilly when they went through what the captain called "Forest Land" and put on a sweatshirt, but she didn't seem to need it anymore.

"I wonder if there is a pool somewhere on the deck. Maybe we should look around. I would like to go for a swim," Jessa said, interrupting the long silence between the three of them.

Anita appeared at her side. "I can show you the way to the bathrooms if you prefer to put on suitable clothing for water activities?"

"Sure! Is there a pool?" Jessa asked.

Teagan pulled at her arm. "Jessa, don't leave your luggage behind—take it with you."

"There will be water activities in Water Land," Anita said with a big smile.

"Water Land? Isn't that a bit contradictory?" Jessa asked, but she knew she wasn't going to get an answer as she followed Anita to the restrooms.

Teagan and Micah stayed in their seats and watched the activity around them. Another tray of food passed by and it looked as if it were specifically prepared for the two of them, because it was towered with their favorite foods. Teagan and Micah did not hesitate and dug into the food before them.

The Thornbergs seemed to be entertaining Jack and Malorey rather well, so Teagan and Micah began to relax a little bit more. Their bellies were full when Jessa returned with a sarong wrapped around her to discreetly cover her swimsuit. She had her rope wrapped around her waist again, as Anita insisted she have it with her at all times. Jessa sat down and saw the food tray and picked up a chocolate iced donut, while at the same time grabbing a buttery roll.

The Captain came over the intercom again and said, "Desert Land." His voice disappeared as people walked over to the ledge and looked out at the miles and miles of sand. Teagan, Jessa, and Micah stayed in their seats, though they were curious to see what would happen next.

"Well, there aren't any tree trunks for people to grab onto this time," Jessa said more to calm herself than the other two. It seemed all three of them were holding their breath as they came closer to Desert Land.

There were loud gasps as everyone on the ship saw another couple dozen people just grab the ledge of the ship and launch themselves off. Jessa ran after one person that looked intent on jumping over the edge of the ship. She was not able to catch the person in time, but instead got to see over the edge of the ship as the person made a soft landing and began throwing sand in the air, laughed, and then made snow angels in the fine sand. The person looked like he was at home and loved where he was. Jessa stood there completely dumbfounded. Teagan and Micah came up behind her and looked over the ledge of the ship. They were shaking their heads in disbelief.

"Things seem a little crazy huh?" Malorey said, behind her three kids.

"Mom, what the heck is going on?" Teagan asked.

"The Thornbergs were only able to explain some things to us, but it seems like we have signed onto something that is much bigger than we expected," Jack answered for Malorey.

"Well, that makes me feel so much better," Micah said sarcastically. "Care to explain?"

Before Jack or Malorey could go into any further details the Thornbergs called out for them. Jessa sighed in frustration and decided to stay by the railing. Teagan took a chair nearby and dropped her head in her hands. Micah walked over to his parents to get a better explanation.

Anita came up behind Jessa. "Can I get you anything?"

Jessa whirled around. "How about a giant book that explains what the heck we are seeing and what is happening? People are jumping off of this ship left and right the moment we get to 'a land.' And none of the staff seems to be worried or care!"

Anita looked upset by the question and answered cautiously, "Miss Jessa, I am so sorry, there is not a book, and I fear that an explanation will not suffice—but rather inhibit what needs to occur naturally for you. You will learn everything and maybe soon." With that, Anita left Jessa alone to wonder what in the world was going on.

Chapter 3

"Jessa!" Teagan yelled.

"What? Jeeze, you don't have to yell," Jessa responded.

"Apparently I do. I have been trying to get your attention for a long time now," Teagan said.

"Well?" Jessa asked.

"You have been quiet for a while. What's on your mind?" Teagan asked apprehensively.

"I don't know. I'm just trying to figure out what is going on here, but at the same time I feel kind of strange," Jessa answered.

"Strange? How? You are starting to scare me," Teagan responded.

"I hate this. I can't explain what I feel, and that is what we have been hearing since we arrived at The Depot. It is like something is stirring in me, like an anticipation of something amazing. Almost like going home after being away for a long time. Does that make sense?" Jessa tried her best to describe what had started after leaving 'Desert Land' and how it had been growing in intensity ever since.

"The ship never stops, Jessa. It keeps going as people jump off, and it's as if they know what is going to happen before it actually happens. And with you talking like this, I am beginning to think you are going to do something crazy too. Anita has been paying a lot of attention to you now," Teagan said nervously, then added, "Don't forget to have your luggage with you."

"What? Why do I need my luggage with me?" Jessa asked absentmindedly.

"I'm going to get Micah; something isn't right," Teagan said as she walked away, wheeling her luggage behind her.

The sun appeared to finally move in the sky; instead of being directly overhead it was beginning to dip to one side. Jessa could not tell which direction it was setting or if it *was* setting. She was beginning to question everything that had existed in her mind as real. Once this trip was over, she realized how much of an eye opener it would be for what she considered 'normal.' The stirring inside of her was growing stronger and stronger. She couldn't shake the feeling that this really wasn't a roller coaster. If so, it was the longest, most interesting, and scariest roller coaster she had ever been on.

"Jessa what's going on? You have Teagan worried about you," Micah's voice interrupted her thoughts.

"I don't know any more than you guys know," Jessa answered defensively.

Anita came up to the three of them and asked if there was anything she could get them. She was a very sweet young woman. Her smile twitched a little, but otherwise she made no attempts to calm their obvious nerves.

Jessa then asked, "How long has it been since we left The Depot?"

"Two and a half days," Anita answered matter-of-factly.

"What! How can that be? We haven't even seen the sunset. That's impossible."

Micah started to argue as well about how impossible it was unless they were near one of the poles of the earth—and it was far too nice out for it to be the case.

Anita smiled; this was a question she was able to answer for them. "The day is done after each land. We don't see the sun set on that land because we continue forward onto the next, where it is still the middle of the day. Although, it appears Miss Jessa noticed the sun has moved a bit, which means we are getting really close to the next land."

"What's the next land?" Teagan asked.

Before Anita could answer, Jessa whispered as she stared off at nothing but blue sky, "Water Land."

Anita smiled as if she knew something. Micah and Teagan were feeling more uncomfortable. And Jessa just stared off into the distance for a while. The captain broke through the silence that ensued between the three of them and announced, "Water Land." And then it was silent.

Teagan watched in horror as the following events played out in slow motion; Her older sister's eyes caught on something and lit up in delight. Teagan had a feeling, and ran towards her, yelling "Nooooo!!!" but it was too late. Jessa put her hands on the ledge of the ship, and without looking back or hesitating, she jumped. Teagan reached the side of the ship just as her sister plunged deep into the most beautiful expanse of glittering, blue water. Several others did as Jessa did, but Teagan's eyes were transfixed on the activity below.

A mass of boulders jutted out of the water. Other people were lying on those smooth rocks, and they appeared to be enjoying the sun. Hundreds of people were laughing and splashing around in the great big water. Teagan's eyes grew wide as she saw there were more than just people in the water—there were huge fish and killer whales! Teagan yelled at Jessa to watch out; a big fish was coming her way. Tears were beginning to flow from her eyes as she watched her sister swim towards the boulders. Jessa seemed to be in a trance and was going to the boulders for a specific reason.

Micah came up behind Teagan and pulled her into his arms, letting her cry. She felt she had lost her older sister to something they couldn't explain. She was still alive, just no longer with them.

"What is going on, Micah?" Teagan asked her older brother.

"None of this makes sense. I don't know what is going on," Micah answered, trying to be calm by breathing slowly, it did not seem to be working. He only hoped Teagan would not notice.

Teagan couldn't believe that for the first time her older brother, who always had answers, couldn't explain the situation.

She looked up at him with fresh tears. "We have to get her back. How are we going to get her back?"

"I don't think we can, but we will find more answers. We have to," Micah answered.

"What if I lose you, too? What if I watch my family get taken away from me, one by one?" Teagan couldn't stop sobbing

Chapter 4

Micah and Teagan marched over to the Thornbergs and their parents. Both of them were angry, confused, and scared.

"Jessa just jumped over the ledge. Any chance you are willing to explain, now, what is going on?" Micah had trouble not yelling.

"We didn't sign up for this—losing members of our family one by one," Teagan added, tears still streaming down her face.

Malorey and Jack turned around with a startled expression on their faces, and then looked beyond Micah and Teagan. Teagan and Micah turned and saw Anita reach for Jessa's luggage; it appeared she was going to dispose of it. Teagan bolted to the other side of the ship in efforts to save her sister's luggage from the cryptic Anita. Just as Anita's hands wrapped around the handle of the luggage piece, Teagan ripped it out of her grasp and ran back towards the remaining members of her family. She gripped both her luggage and Jessa's.

Mrs. Thornberg finally answered Micah's question, but it wasn't the satisfactory answer they were looking for. "That must be the place she is meant to be. I have heard great things about Water Land."

"Are you serious right now?! We just lost our sister to who-knows-what, and that is all you have to say?!" Micah yelled.

Malorey turned to Mrs. Thornberg and asked for a better explanation. Malorey and Jack were beyond panicked; the trip had gone too far.

Anita came up behind the Robinson's and interrupted what could have been the first real explanation.

"The captain has asked me to accompany you to your seats," Anita said before turning to the Thornbergs. "Mr. and Mrs. Thornberg, the captain would like to speak with you."

"Following you anywhere is the last thing I wanna do," Teagan spat out.

Micah grabbed Teagan's hand and tried to pull her, but she wouldn't budge. She stood by the ledge of the ship and stared out at the expanse of nothing, clutching the two pieces of luggage. Micah left her to take his seat next to his parents. Teagan didn't know how much actual time had passed, but the Captain's voice came over the intercom again: "Cold Land."

Teagan felt a blast of cold air just as the intercom went silent. In defiance, she did not look around to see if anyone was jumping off. She knew her family would not jump over the edge; they were from Minnesota and had their share of cold. Her efforts to ignore the people jumping off the ship were in vain as she saw several people land in powdery, white snow and run off. She got a chill, and felt powerless about the events that were taking place. It didn't help that no one would offer an explanation.

Teagan wondered how Jessa was, if she was okay, and if she had already forgotten about her family. Teagan knew she still had her mom, dad, and Micah, but if felt lonely where she was standing.

Jessa couldn't explain what happened even if she had the dictionary in front of her with the best choice words at her disposal. As she climbed up a smooth boulder and sat down on a ledge watching the people splashing and laughing, she replayed what happened in her mind. She remembered looking over the ledge of the boat and seeing the most magnificent blue water, glittering and inviting.

She loved swimming and would spend days at the beach during the summer. But something, more like someone, caught her eye and it was that which sent her over the edge without looking back. It felt like she was being tugged along in a trance towards this beautiful man. When she first spotted him, he was jumping off one of the higher boulders into the water. She didn't even know what he looked like up close, but she couldn't stop herself from going in the direction of where she last saw him. She was unable to find him, which was why she was now perched on the boulder scanning the water.

"Looking for me?" a voice behind her asked. That voice sounded like nothing she had ever heard before; it resonated deep within and shook her to her core. It was a strong male voice, with a slight accent. She turned around slowly and saw the beautiful figure standing just above her on another ledge of the boulder. He took her breath away. Apparently she did the same to him, because she could hear his own breathing stop for a moment.

"Umm, yes?" Jessa answered, confused, and then shook her head at how ridiculous she must have sounded.

"I've been waiting for you," the man said.

"You have?" Jessa tried not to sound flattered that such a gorgeous person would be waiting for her.

"Of course," he chuckled.

"H-h-how could you be waiting for me? I don't even know you," Jessa stammered.

"I just had a feeling," He answered.

Jessa still couldn't believe what she was looking at. His muscles bunched in places that suggested he worked out, however there were no signs of a fitness center in the area. His sandy blond hair just barely touched his shoulders, and his eyes were a dark blue. He had a hard look to his face, but it was easily softened by his perfect smile. Jessa figured there had to be some explanation for this entire journey, and was hoping he would help. At the moment she didn't worry too much about it, but she was hopeful that he could answer some of her questions.

"What's your name?" Jessa asked.

"Tristan. Yours?" he responded.

"My name is Jessa—well, Janessa Avery Robinson. I like your name," Jessa responded.

"Janessa, but you prefer Jessa?" he distracted her with his question.

"Yes, I do. Can you please explain to me what is going on?" She said as he moved to sit next to her.

"That's a pretty vague question. I'm not sure how to answer it," Tristan said evasively.

"No one on the ship would explain what this place is, and I am struggling with whether or not this is even real." Jessa threw up her arms in exasperation.

"It is real. What would you like to understand?" He asked calmly. The gravity of what she had done moments before meeting Tristan was slowly sinking in piece by piece. She could not believe how impulsive she was; jumping off of a ship in just her sarong and swimsuit, without her luggage or a goodbye to her family. She didn't even know when she would see them again. Worrying about some explanation of this entire journey should be the last of her problems, but it seemed to be the key to them.

She dropped her head in her hands, overwhelmed with everything around her, while sounds of splashing and laughing echoed off the boulders. When she finally lifted her head, she realized Tristan had not taken his eyes off of her—he looked worried for her. Jessa struggled under his gaze and turned towards the sparkling water and watched for a long moment, taking in her surroundings.

Jessa tried to wrap her mind around everything surrounding her. Questions continued to assail her, ones that she didn't think would be answered. She was frustrated; everyone below seemed content with not knowing what was going on. Then she wondered if they did know and she was the only one left out.

Jessa had startled Tristan when she yelled out: "What the heck is happening here!?"

"Jessa, what is wrong?" Tristan asked.

"Everything is wrong. Where is my family? Why aren't they here with me? Are they stuck on that ship?" she said in frustration.

"Are any of them in the water or on the boulders?" he asked.

Jessa scanned the water for several long moments, looking at faces in anticipation of seeing someone she knew. She continued to wait, making sure she looked at everyone just in case they were underwater. She shuttered and let out a long shaky breath as her fear was confirmed: they weren't here.

"Where would they be?" Jessa asked quietly.

Tristan almost didn't hear her with the noises going on around them, but answered, "Most likely on the ship or one of the Lands."

A breeze rustled her long, brown hair as she sat and stared at Tristan. She noticed that he wore swim trunks that were rather popular from where she came from, but he had an aged leather pouch on his waist, held there by a rope, much like the rope she had around her waist. It was an odd combination of trendy shorts and aged leather. She allowed her mind to muddle over that for a while. The sun was moving even further down on the horizon, and she remembered what Anita said about the days starting over after leaving each land.

"How many 'Lands' are there?" Jessa asked after a long silence.

He stared off at nothing in particular, seeming to allow her question to swim around in his brain. Jessa started to get impatient and tried for a different question.

"Were you brought here by the ship?" Jessa asked and cleared her throat, realizing that he might not answer any of her questions.

"No, I was born here. My parents were brought by

the ship many suns ago and have lived here ever since. The captain was really happy about my birth. Anyone that is born in the Lands is cherished," Tristan answered.

"How many Lands are there?" Jessa repeated her question.

"Fifteen," Tristan said as he looked out into the ocean.

Jessa sat up. "*Fifteen*?! And what are they? Where are they?"

"I only know based on what I have heard. I might not even know the right name for them. There is Forest Land, Desert Land, Water Land, Mythical Land, Edible Land, Cold Land, Safari Land, Swamp Land, Colors Land, Tech. Land, Dinosaur Land, Music Land, Valley Land, Beneath Land, and The Oracle—which, the last one technically isn't a Land." He ticked off the different places with his fingers.

"I've only seen three; I have twelve more that I need to see?" Jessa said.

"*No!*" Tristan yelled; the urgency in his voice startled Jessa so much she almost fell back in the water.

"What? Why? I have to go—my family is still on that ship and I didn't even say goodbye. I don't even know when I will see them again, or if I will," Jessa responded.

"They might not be on the ship anymore. It is possible they have already reached the Land they belong in." Tristan explained.

"Would they all be at the same place and I just ditched my family?" Jessa's worry was increasing.

"I doubt it. It's possible. It's more likely they each belong to a different Land. Please don't go," Tristan answered.

"I have to go. I have to find my family," Jessa said, though she was sad she had to leave.

"Alright. When are we going?" Tristan sighed in frustration.

"We? There is no 'we.' I will go by myself," Jessa responded.

"We are mated. I belong to you and you to me; I have to go everywhere you go. I need to protect you; that is my role," Tristan said.

"*Mated*?! What does *that* mean?" Jessa asked. "I only just met you."

"You jumped off the ship because this is where you

44

belong, and you chose me," Tristan tried to explain.

Jessa felt like she was losing her mind; the more she was learning the more confused she got. She ran a hand through her damp hair in frustration.

"How long do I belong here? Because I have a home, school, work, and dishes piled up in the sink— meaning I have a life to get back to," Jessa said, even though she has never felt she belonged anywhere as strongly as she had at that moment.

"I was hoping forever, but—" Tristan started to say.

"*Forever!*" Jessa said.

"Maybe we should talk about something else?" Tristan offered.

Just as Jessa was about to argue, she saw movement in the water. Then she saw a shadow about the size of a decent-sized boat under the surface of the water. After a moment, she saw a dorsal fin breach the water. To her terrified amazement, a large killer whale came up to the boulders and sprayed water all over the two of them.

"There are people swimming with killer whales!" Jessa looked horrified and awed at the same time.

"Here, they are our protectors. We each get one. I

have one, and if you jump back in the water and stay there long enough, the one that was made for you will start swimming this way," Tristan said.

"Protectors from what? If I touch the water it will come here?" Jessa asked.

"Each Land has a danger that it faces and with that come a protector and a mate. I am your mate as well as a protector, but your killer whale will protect you from dangers in the water that I cannot. There are creatures in this water that are extremely dangerous; we have lost many people and killer whales to these creatures. They are bigger than the ship that you came on. And yes, if you are in the water long enough, it sends a pulse to the whale and they travel to where you are," Tristan answered.

"How is it possible that the more answers I get, the more confused I am? How do I get back to the ship?" Jessa figured that was the only solution to this situation.

Tristan put his hand under Jessa's chin and forced her to look into his bright, blue eyes. "Why do you want to go back to the ship?"

"Because my family is there. The way you described it, there are things that I should be afraid of, and I don't like being afraid. I jumped in that water without even thinking; it was automatic. I don't have anything I need with me...my curling iron, clothes, my makeup! Holy crap, my makeup!" Jessa was beginning to panic.

"From my point of view, you don't need any makeup. And if you really must go, I will go with you. The rope brings you back to the ship," Tristan said sadly.

"Okay," Jessa said, starting to calm down.

"Before we go, would you like to see where we live?" Tristan said, trying his best to postpone leaving.

"I suppose," Jessa said.

Jessa couldn't help but wonder if her family was worrying about her. Surely Teagan was flipping out. She hoped she could return to the ship soon to reassure them that she was okay.

Chapter 5

"Micah!" Teagan yelled.

"What? Jeeze, you don't need to yell," Micah said from his spot by the ledge of the ship.

He had stood up after seeing people jumping off the ship left and right. He had hoped he could get used to what happened when each land was announced, but he hadn't. They had passed through quite a few lands by this time, and he was really curious about Edible Land. He thought it sounded like something out of *Willie Wonka and the Chocolate Factory*.

"Apparently I do have to yell, since I have said your name several times now," Teagan said. She froze as she remembered that was pretty close to the same thing she said before Jessa jumped over the ledge of the ship.

Anita was close by Micah, offering to help with anything. This only made Teagan more nervous. She ran up to Micah and held onto him.

"Please don't leave me," Teagan said.

"What are you talking about? Like all those crazies that have been jumping off the ship? Don't worry," Micah said.

"One of those crazies was Jessa," Teagan reasoned.

"What did you think of Colors Land?" Micah asked, trying to change the subject.

"It was beautiful; everything was lit up with so many shades of colors. It was no wonder that we lost about half of the people on the ship to that land. And Edible Land took a lot of people that obviously like food," Teagan chuckled.

Chapter 6

Tristan stood up and held out his hand. Jessa took hold and realized how quickly she felt she could trust him. They climbed to the top of the boulders, which was not as easy as Tristan made it look—on several occasions he had to keep her from falling. Her hands were getting scuffed up from some of the ragged edges, and she could feel a bruise forming on her shin from one of the times she slipped. Once they reached the top she saw a beautiful Island that, for some odd reason, she had been unable to see when she was on the ship.

"How come I never saw this from the ship?" Jessa asked.

"With all the Lands, our homes are not seen from the ship," Tristan said.

Jessa remembered Forest Land and how the people just grabbed onto the fallen logs in the ravine and ran into the forest; she was not able to see a home there, but she was curious what it looked like. She remembered the Desert Land and how there was nothing but sand in sight.

She stood there, looking at the island; it looked like a postcard. It was difficult for her to believe it was real, but she reasoned that it wasn't the first time that she had struggled with that. Before they left the top of the boulders, Jessa decided she wanted to know a little bit more about Tristan.

"So what is in that pouch that you carry around?" Jessa asked.

"These are the things that are important to me. I can make you one if you want," Tristan offered.

"That is very sweet of you. My luggage carries the things that are important to me, so when I get back to the ship I can get that," Jessa said.

"What good are those earthly things here? We don't have electricity, although it does sound amazing the way that my father described it. And makeup is such a waste when it covers up what is already beautiful. I can make you a pouch to carry the things you treasure here," Tristan argued.

Jessa felt as though Tristan was getting more and more frustrated at her desire to be back on the ship. She had an unexplainable feeling of belonging, but there was also a curiosity to see the other lands and a need to be with her family. She wondered if she made her decision too hastily.

"Tristan, I'm not trying to make you upset. I just, I guess I am just trying to figure things out. This isn't normal…what you are, where you live, what you do—my mind cannot wrap around this stuff," Jessa explained.

"I've never known someone to ask so many questions," Tristan said quietly.

"Probably because I don't believe in any of this stuff. I'm not a little kid with a wild imagination anymore. I believe I will wake up tomorrow morning in my bed," Jessa stated.

"Well, you don't have to believe when it can easily be proven. You stay here for one day and wake up tomorrow morning and see where you are. How does that sound?" Tristan offered.

"I don't see why not. How about a tour of your place? Where is your house?" Jessa said as she looked at the island.

"House? I don't have a house. I will show you where I normally sleep though," Tristan answered. Jessa frowned, not liking the sound of that.

Tristan continued: "You ready?" He grabbed her hand and waited for her to nod. He counted to three and pulled her with him as they soared off the top of the boulders and plunged deep into the water. Jessa did not expect that; she thought they would climb down. When she came up from the water, she was sputtering and splashing in shock at how exhilarating it was.

They were wading in the water for only a few moments when a killer whale came right up to Tristan. He introduced Jessa to Niko, his protector. Then he grabbed onto the whale's fin and Jessa's hand, and he pulled her up on Niko's back. They made it to the island a lot quicker than if they would have swam there themselves. The waves pushed them up on the sandy beach; the sand was so fine and smooth in Jessa's hands. She wanted to sit there and build a sand castle while the waves touched her feet, but Tristan quickly grabbed her up and dragged her away from the water.

"What's the rush?" Jessa asked indignantly.

"If you don't want to stay here then maybe it's best if your protector doesn't come for you. The longer you are in the water, the higher the chance is that the whale will feel the pulse," Tristan tried to explain.

"So I get a 'mate' and a killer whale. Do I get to name the whale?" Jessa teased.

"Yes," he answered, but it was laced with a bit of frustration.

"Hey, what's wrong? What did I do?" Jessa asked.

"It's just frustrating answering all of your questions when you don't plan on staying here. And I have to go with you," Tristan answered.

"You can stay; I'm not making you go," Jessa defended.

"No, I can't. I have to go with you; I do not have a choice. I am your mate and your protector," Tristan said again.

"Whoa, man, it's not like we're married. Even then you have your own choices." Jessa put her hands up in surrender.

"Is that an earth thing?" Tristan asked.

"You refer to earth as if it is a faraway place. Yes, that is an earth thing—in most places. Equal rights," Jessa answered.

Tristan walked towards some high palm trees and the center of the island. Jessa had no choice but to follow him, even in his angry state since she was not familiar with the area and did not want to be left alone. She marveled at the amount of vegetation there was; the ground was difficult to see with all the plant life. She enjoyed the smell of the ocean and the mixture of the rainforest that occupied the island. As they traveled further into the island, the darker it got. While she was walking behind Tristan, being mindful of her steps with her bare feet, something flew right over her head.

"What the heck was that?" Jessa yelled.

"Snake," Tristan answered.

"You were trying to throw a snake at me? Seriously!" Jessa stopped in her tracks to make her point known.

He turned toward her. "I was throwing it out of your way so you wouldn't get hurt; I did not throw it at you. You seriously think that I would throw a snake at you? You are the most difficult woman I have ever…" Tristan stopped mid-sentence and then turned to continue down a narrow path. Jessa quickly caught up.

"How am I the most difficult woman? What did I do?" Jessa asked. "We just met."

"You think I would put you in danger, when I made it clear that I am going to protect you," Tristan argued.

"Just because I want to leave, that makes me the most difficult woman you ever…ever what?" Jessa asked.

A long silence came before Tristan finally answered, and he answered quietly: "Ever mated."

"Wait, hold up. You've been mated before? I am not the first person you have been mated to? Wait a second, are you mated to more than one at a time or something? Do I need to mark my territory or something?" Jessa was starting to join him in anger, and she was having an odd sense of jealousy. She instantly flushed at her last question, knowing it made her sound like a jealous girlfriend.

She didn't understand why she was already experiencing those feelings. Jessa had to mentally tell herself to settle down; she had only met him a couple of hours ago. It seemed as if they were a couple, and arguing already; she felt like she had known him longer than a couple of hours. Before Tristan could answer the first question, she was thinking of a few others to add.

"Yes I was mated before. No, we are not mated to more than one person at a time, so there will be no 'territory marking.' You have me whether you want me or not," Tristan answered.

"I did want you," Jessa said so softly she didn't think he could hear her.

Tristan stopped in his tracks, but didn't turn around,

and said in a sad voice, "That sounds very past tense." Without waiting for a response, he continued forward. He didn't want to hear one.

"What happened to your previous mate? That sounds past tense to me, too," Jessa countered.

Tristan didn't feel like answering the question. He continued down an unmarked path. In his mind, he was shaking his head at the entire situation. When he first saw her on the ledge of the ship, he couldn't believe how beautiful she was. He was excited to get a chance to learn more about her—so excited that he didn't waste time and went right up to her. He had no idea that this young woman would be even more beautiful up close; he also didn't know how frustrating she could be with her quick desire to leave. He had no idea why anyone would want to leave almost as soon as she had arrived. This was home to him.

Jessa replayed the entire trip over in her had as they trudged through the forest. She noticed the many different sounds from animals she was sure were scary. Trees towered over them for what seemed like miles. The large leaves that covered the different layers of the forest were all different shapes and sizes. Bugs were fighting for an opportunity to bite her as she swatted them away numerous times. As soon as they had entered the forest, she felt she could drink the moisture in the air.

Tristan turned their conversations over in his head to figure out where it all went wrong. He chastised himself for not being more patient with her. She was in a world she didn't know existed and had no preparation for what she was seeing. Even though it had bits and pieces that were exactly like earth, there were several things that were not. She had yet to see them since she jumped into the water, but she got a glimpse when she was on the ship.

He promised himself he would try to be more patient. He realized his earnest desire to have and hold her were clouding his ability to remain calm when she appeared to want nothing to do with him or the land he had called home his entire life. It was hard not to be offended and defensive. He remained quiet for the rest of their walk so he could get a grip on his temper.

It seemed like they had been walking for a while. Jessa was beginning to feel sores and aches in her feet. She was just about to say something when they stopped in the middle of the dense rainforest. Tristan turned to the right and lifted a large leaf that covered a hole in the ground about 2 feet in diameter. He held the leaf and offered his hand to Jessa.

She wasn't sure what was in that hole, but she didn't think he would deliberately put her danger—no matter how upset he was. She grabbed his hand and he grabbed her other hand and dangled her over the hole like she weighed nothing before slowly lowering her down. It was darker in the hole than it was in the rainforest, and Jessa could see nothing.

"A flashlight would be perfect right now," Jessa muttered to herself. She realized that was the first sound she had made since asking him about his mate.

Tristan jumped down after her, and then a light shown from a necklace around Tristan's neck that she had not seen there before. It illuminated the small space. The underground pseudo cave was just big enough to fit two people comfortably lying down, with a small area to sit in was off to the side.

She looked around and saw that the place must have been dug out. It smelled musty and moisture was locked in. She could feel her skin was clammy, even though it was a little chilly. Obviously there wasn't anything hanging on the dirt walls. Jessa had no idea how the place hadn't caved in yet. She figured one rainstorm would wipe it out.

"This is my home. I built it myself," Tristan said with pride.

"How long have you lived here?" Jessa asked.

"Since I was old enough to go to the ocean," Tristan answered.

"How old were you then?" Jessa pushed further, trying to get a better answer.

"My mother taught me a little about your method of keeping track of age, but I don't remember it so well...I think it was 15 years old?" Tristan shrugged.

"Did you pull that out of your pouch?" Jessa gestured towards the necklace.

"Yes; it helps to see down here. We have many of these glowing stones. We found them in a cave on the other side of the island," Tristan answered.

Jessa couldn't fight the feeling that even though she had only met him that day, they were already drifting apart. His responses were short and stiff. It was a foolish feeling, since she barely knew him, but it seemed his response was emotionless.

"So you have never left this place, and you aren't the least bit curious of the other lands? I am so curious about Edible Land—I mean, what does that even mean? Is the land edible, or does it eat you, or…" Jessa was talking to fill the silence.

"I'm not curious about it, because I have already been told about them, and I love everything about this place. Everyone I love is here, too," Tristan cut her off.

"Okay. So tell me about it. What is Edible Land?" Jessa asked as she took a seat on the cold, damp, dirt floor.

Tristan had made his house deep enough so he could stand up straight. He ran a hand through his hair; he looked like he was struggling with whether or not he should tell her. There was a long silence.

"Fine, nevermind...forget I asked." Jessa got up and made her way to the exit and then turned around. "In efforts to not ruin your home how do you prefer me to get out of here?"

"I made a stepladder—it is next to the entrance," Tristan answered.

She internally fought with the fact that he had little difficulty with her just leaving him. She didn't want to leave, but she couldn't stay in his quiet presence; it made her nervous. It was too late now for her to go back on her actions, so she turned toward the opening.

Jessa felt around for the ladder and put it next to the entrance to climb out of his little home. Once she made it out, she laid down on her stomach so that she could reach down and put the ladder back. She wasn't happy about getting dirt all over her sarong, which was still plastered to her body, but she didn't want to be rude and just leave without putting it back where she found it.

She then stood up, looked around, and went back the way they came—at least, she hoped it was the way they came. Tristan did not follow her, and she couldn't decide if she wanted or expected him to. The further she walked, the quicker she realized she might need his help in navigating the rainforest. She stood there for a while, trying to decide which way to go, and trying to hear the ocean. All she could hear were the loud sounds of the creatures that lived in the rainforest. Then it began to rain; an instant downpour. The rain was chilly, and she just stood there and began to shake.

She didn't know if it was lack of sleep or the impact of the entire day, but tears started streaming down her face. She was thankful that no one would be able to see the tears as they teamed up with the rain on her cheeks. She couldn't stop and the tears turned to sobs. She fell to her knees, her face in her hands. She couldn't believe what had happened in the few days since they left Minnesota; everything went from normal to completely unexplainable and unnatural.

After a while, she stood up and tried to brush off the dirt, but it had long since become mud with the rain. She would make it to the beach; somehow, she would get there. She was just about to take a step forward, when a voice said, "You're going the wrong way."

Tristan appeared right in front of her. The rain must have drowned out the sound of his footsteps.

"All I want to do is get to the beach. Just point me in

that direction and then you don't have to bother with me anymore," Jessa said, trying to cover the quiver in her voice.

"Why are you crying?" Tristan asked.

"I'm not," Jessa lied. There was no way for him to really tell with the rain.

"Yes, you are. Your tears are purple," Tristan said.

"What?" Jessa asked as she lifted her hand to her face and pulled her hand away; she was startled to see a light purple splash in her hand. The rain quickly washed it away.

"Why are you crying?" Tristan repeated.

"Please, just point me in the direction of the beach," Jessa said, no longer trying to cover her tears.

"I will bring you there," Tristan said, and led the way.

Silently, they trudged through the rain forest; a few times, Tristan had thrown some snakes away from them. When they finally reached the beach, Jessa was surprised to it was still sunny, although the sun was still slowly descending in the horizon.

"The rope that you were given will bring you back to the ship. You have to hold it a certain way. And when you do, you will have to grip my hand tightly, because the pull to the ship is powerful. You cannot lose your grip on the rope or me when we go…so be prepared for a jolt. It should be a matter of seconds before we are on board, wherever the ship is on its journey. It is possible that it is several lands ahead by now," Tristan explained as he used a vine to show her how to hold the rope. When he was done demonstrating, he dropped the vine. He grabbed her hand, squeezed his eyes shut, and braced himself for the pull.

"I'm not going. Not now, anyways," Jessa answered and removed her hand from his grip. She sat down and watched the waves, allowing the rhythm of each wave to slowly soothe her.

"If there is no reason for you to stay here, then why wait?" Tristan asked as he sat down next to her.

"I think you misunderstood me. There are several reasons to stay here. There are only a few reasons for me to go, but those reasons are my family. I have an older brother, Micah, who is 24, and my sister— Teagan—she is 18, and my parents, Malorey and Jack. They are probably worried sick about me. I did not mean for you to think that I didn't want to be here. I think I must be tired, because I can't seem to get a grip on my emotions," Jessa explained as more tears spilled down her cheeks.

"As beautiful as your tears are, they are nothing compared to the beauty of your face when you are smiling. How can I make them stop?" Tristan said.

"Does everyone have different colored tears here?" Jessa asked, not knowing how to take the compliment.

"I have only seen a few people cry here, and yes, their tears are a different color than yours. But their tears are green; everyone's tears here are green," Tristan answered.

"What color were your previous mate's tears?" Jessa asked with a bit of anger; for some reason, she wanted to see if she was special compared to his previous mate.

"I never saw her cry. I wasn't mated to her long before she was taken away from me. The creature got her before I even showed her my home. So there is nothing to be jealous of, if that is what you are feeling," Tristan said.

"I'm sorry about your other mate. But I'm not jealous," Jessa lied.

In efforts to change the subject, Jessa asked about the pouch again. This time Tristan slipped it off the rope and dropped it into her hands. Inside she found a perfect seashell—when she put it to her ear she could hear the ocean—the necklace that he had worn in his home, a bracelet, a small water canteen, a knife, and another seashell. He sat, silent and still, as she went over every piece, inspecting and touching. He watched her facial expressions. The whole experience was uncomfortable for him; he felt vulnerable with her inspecting his private possessions. He gave her only one instruction, to not let the sun touch the necklace and to leave it in the pouch. She had so many questions but could tell he was wary with her just holding his things. She handed the pouch back.

"Thank you for allowing me to see what is most important to you," Jessa whispered.

"Don't you want to know about them?" Tristan asked.

"When you are ready to tell me about them, I will listen," Jessa said.

Teagan hovered near Micah by the ledge of the ship. She could tell he was becoming more and more distant. Anita was getting excited and doing her best to be accommodating, however it was only stirring anxiety in Teagan. Micah hadn't said a word since they talked about Colors Land and Edible Land, and his silence was killing her.

"What's going on, Micah?" She asked as she touched his arm. She could feel how tightly strung his muscles were, as if he was gripping the side of the ship with all his might.

"I don't know. I can't explain it. Something isn't right," Micah answered and then turned to Teagan. "I'm trying to fight against something that I don't even know, but it's pulling me. The more the ship moves forward, the harder it pulls," Micah said, fear laced in his voice.

"Micah, please, please don't leave me!" Teagan said as she gripped his arm even tighter.

"I'm trying to stay, I am...can't you tell?" Micah said with exhaustion.

Anita came up to Teagan and said in a sweet voice, "Miss Robinson, you must let go of young Mr. Robinson. It seems that he must go soon."

"Are you out of your freaking mind? I'm not losing any more of my family to this crazy ride!" Teagan yelled.

The captain's voice came over the intercom again: "Tech. Land."

"I'm really beginning to hate when he speaks," Teagan seethed.

Her hold on Micah was not strong enough. She felt, more than she saw, him leave her presence. She was battling with Anita and distracted by the captain's and didn't notice her grip loosen on Micah. She turned around as she saw the back of his head go over the edge of the ship. She screamed and yelled for him; she gripped the air, hoping there was some way that she could get him to come back. He was gone.

She kept screaming until she didn't have much of a voice left. Tears were staining her cheeks as she shook her head in disbelief. Anita gently grabbed Teagan's shoulders, only to have her hands thrown off. Teagan sunk to the deck and tried to find a way to breathe right.

Two more lands had passed before she was able to gain enough strength to stand back up. Once she was on her feet, she marched in the direction of what she assumed was the captain's quarters. Anita stopped her and tried to reason with her before she made a mistake.

"Miss Robinson, please don't," Anita pleaded.

"Oh, yeah? Just how many family members do I have to lose before you think I'm going to do something about it?" Teagan asked.

"You haven't lost them. They just found their place; you need to find yours," Anita tried to explain.

"My place. What the heck does that mean? What is this pull that everyone seems to be talking about or clearly experiencing when they jump off a moving ship?!" Teagan was starting to yell.

Anita was about to say something, but Teagan rushed past her, back toward her parents. She was running in full panic mode. She saw both of her parents holding onto the railing on the edge of the ship. She hadn't realized that they were coming upon another land. The captain's voice came over the intercom: "Valley Land."

Those words were fuel to her as pushed forward. She was running faster than she had ever run before. Her feet pounded on the wood planks of the deck and sweat was streaking down her back as her body used every ounce of power to move forward. Teagan was trying to scream, but she was already losing her voice a second time from yelling at Anita.

"Noooo! Don't leave me!" Teagan tried to yell out. Her mother looked back just as the Thornbergs pulled her and Jack over the ledge with them.

Teagan was only a few yards away and she just stood in that spot, paralyzed. She couldn't think straight. Her entire family had just abandoned ship during this trip. This was the longest, most detailed nightmare she had ever experienced. She told herself that she had to wake up if it was a nightmare. She desperately wanted to wake up.

The waves continued to rush up on the sandy beach. In the background, Jessa could swear she heard laughter and splashing still taking place at the boulders where she first jumped in. After a couple of hours of lying out on the sand and making a sand castle, she was getting a little thirsty. She asked Tristan for some water from his canteen, and he delighted in being able to provide for her. He had helped her with the sand castle and it looked like a great masterpiece by the time they finished.

Jessa was enjoying the simplicity and joy of building a sand castle and actually having the time to complete it when she heard a loud, piercing sound. She listened more closely; it seemed to be screaming.

"What was that?" Jessa stood up.

"Oh, no!" Tristan said as he jumped up. "The creature. All those people!" Tristan started running towards the water.

Jessa chased him. "Tristan, what's going on?"

"I'll explain later. I have to go. Stay right here," Tristan said.

"You are kidding me right?" Jessa yelled.

"I won't die. Please just stay here. More people are going to die the longer I stay to explain things to you," Tristan said, trying to shake her off of him so he could get Niko and fight.

"You can't just leave me here!" Jessa yelled as he took off into the water.

Jessa paced the beach. She could hear more screams coming from beyond the boulders, and they rang in her ears. She didn't even see Niko or Tristan, because he quickly disappeared under the water. What she did see, she would never be able to take from her mind. A towering shadow came up over the boulders and slapped at them, forcing people to fall. She could see the boulders shake from the creature's power. A blood-curdling sound ripped through her throat as she screamed in horror at what she saw.

Tristan was not exaggerating the size of the creature; it was huge, slimy, and black. The shadowing creature had slime dripping from everywhere along its large, scaled body, so much so that she was able to see it from her spot on the beach. Looking around to see if there was anything she could use as a weapon was a waste since it was only sand and seashells that surrounded her. Finally, she ran back to the tree line, grabbed a long, bamboo stick, and headed for the water. She didn't have a knife but she could try to pierce the creature. She didn't want to admit that she was making a really stupid decision.

Jessa paused only for a moment before stepping into the water. Was it true—would she get a killer whale too? Another scream broke her train of thought and spurred her forward. She trudged through the water, having no idea if she would even make it the distance to the boulders or if she would make it in time. She put the bamboo stick in the back of her sarong and tightly wrapped it up, using her sarong as more of a sash than what it was intended for. She did the front crawl for a while and then switched to the breast-stroke until she realized she was quickly running out of steam.

The waves were much more powerful than before. Panic struck when she realized she wasn't even half-way to the boulders. Big waves came down over her head and forced her body into a twirl underwater. This made it difficult for her to know which way was up. She swallowed more saltwater than she cared to in a lifetime. One time she swallowed so much saltwater that she threw up right in the water. Not one of her prouder moments. She shook her head, trying to get her bearings. All that time in the water and playing in the ocean didn't help one bit. Of course, she usually had a surf board.

Another wave took her under, and Jessa kicked, hoping she was kicking in the right direction. Her powerful kicks eventually pushed her to the surface and reminded her just why she liked the water so much. She felt as if she could defy gravity, floating on the surface and gliding along. She was able to draw from that thought and push herself forward even when the odds were against her. She knew that most people found the ocean scary, but for some reason she never saw it that way. She knew she was out of her league with the creature and was hoping to come up with a solid plan by the time she got to the boulders.

Another scream ripped from the other side of the boulders. Her muscles were being tested and when there was only a third of the way left to go, they were warning her not to push any further. Her movements were slowing, even though her mind kept shouting to move forward. Eventually, she noticed she wasn't moving forward at all. She was barely treading water. The waves were still large; she assumed they were from the mess the creature was making. Her head bobbed in and out of the water. She swallowed some more saltwater and it burned her throat. She bounced up a couple of times, coughing the entire time. It did not give her the air she desperately needed before being pushed underwater again. She tried to get her arms to cooperate. She didn't panic like many people do when faced with the possibility of dying. The last thought that went through her mind before her head dipped underwater and she began to sink was, "All those people…All those people."

Chapter 7

Jessa saw the surface of the water get further and further away from her. Something bumped her, and she felt a swift movement beneath her. The surface of the water was coming quickly into view. She broke the surface with a loud gasp and more coughing. After several long moments and even more attempts to get a deep breath, she noticed she was sitting in the water—still a third of the way from the boulders. She had trouble wrapping her head around that and wondered what had just happened. Was there was an air pocket that shot her up? And what was she sitting on? Jessa looked down and at the same time felt the rubbery skin of a killer whale just beneath her.

She continued to rub her hands along the unusual texture and realized she wasn't afraid; she felt comforted and safe. She knew the whale was not Niko, and she wondered if it was someone else's whale. Surely it wasn't hers, since she had only been in the water for a few moments. Was that all it took? The questions had to wait as she urged the beast underneath her to move forward. The killer whale did not move. She tried to talk to the whale and realized she could only croak. "Come on, let's get into the action. We have to save those people." It was hard with all the saltwater that she had swallowed. The whale would not follow her instruction, and was bringing her back to the island.

"No, come on, wrong way!" Jessa yelled. She gave up trying to get the whale to do her bidding since she obviously did not know how to speak the language. Barely getting a renewed strength from sitting on the whale, she felt as though she could at least try to make it to the boulders again, so she jumped off the back of the whale and hoped it didn't bite her for jumping off of its back.

She pushed her way through the water like she had before. She had no idea why she was trying anymore when the screaming seemed to die down and she didn't know how to fight, but something kept pushing her forward—something from within. It didn't take long for her to notice the whale was right next to her side. She was tempted more than once to grab onto the fin to get an extra pull, but she resisted because she feared that the whale would bring her back to the island and all the work she did would be wasted.

The moment her hands touched the cold stone of one of the boulders, she breathed a sigh of relief, even though waves were slapping her up against the stone. She tried to climb the boulder but could not get a hold. At about the third try, she looked over at the whale. "A little boost, please? It's obvious I'm not going back to the island without at least trying to help."

At that, the whale went under the water, placed its snout under her feet, and lifted up. Jessa shot out of the water and landed straight on the boulder. She gained her balance, took a moment, and started climbing the boulders. Her muscles were shaking and protesting against every movement. She pushed herself up the boulders and got angry with herself for not thinking this through. She was not cut out to swim miles, climb boulders, or see what was surely waiting for her on the other side of the wall of boulders.

Jessa had slipped several times, so her skinned knees and scraped hands left her a little physically vulnerable when she got to the top; what she saw when she reached the top left her emotionally vulnerable. The water on the other side of the boulders was thick with slime, a dark red color, and pieces of bodies and dead fish were everywhere. The creature was not in the area anymore, but she could see a black shadow swimming away—its size made it easy to conclude that it was the creature. A breeze picked up and pushed Jessa's long, brown out of her face even though it was still wet. The wind carried the scent of death and pain.

She stood on the top of the boulders. Any observer would see a warrior in her stance, but if they looked at her eyes they would see a softness about her. Tears streamed, unyielding, down her face, and drops would even make it down to the water below. She looked down and saw the purple tears. The water below began to turn instantly back to the sparkling blue water, removing any remnant of red and pain that was there only moments before. Jessa couldn't believe what she had seen and what she was seeing now. It wasn't long before the red was completely gone.

All at once, she lost strength to hold herself up and sat down at the top of the boulders. Her mind rolled over the things she had seen. Drawing her legs up and curling into herself, she stared off into the never-ending water. There was an emptiness creeping into her, as she realized people died and she couldn't do anything about it. She recalled how angry and depressed she would get about the pain and suffering she saw on television back home or when she saw commercials to adopt a little child from another country.

Those thoughts brought her back to her home and

the present feeling of how out of place she felt here. Just like back home, she felt useless; she despised that feeling and was even more desperate to change it. The desire to change lives, help people, and make a difference only grew. Helplessness was a feeling she refused to have again, and she would do whatever she could to learn to defend others and fight for them.

She did not know how long she was there, and could not recall all the thoughts that went through her mind. She remembered thinking to herself that these were the kind of images reserved for horror movies. How could anyone sleep at night with the images of the creature swimming in their thoughts, she wondered.

She settled her face in her hands as tears continued to stream down her cheeks, as if they had a mind of their own. The sting of raw flesh from climbing the rocks was not lost on her, which brought to her attention the strange, quick relief that came so quickly, as if her hands didn't hurt anymore. She dropped her hands from her face and looked down at them. She couldn't believe what she was seeing; her hands were knitting together and healing right before her eyes. Jessa chuckled a little at herself as she realized how many unbelievable things surrounded her. It made sense there was a quicker healing rate in a land where danger was all around them.

She looked at her knees and wondered why they were

taking longer to heal than her hands, as well as other areas that met their fate at the hands of the boulders. Her burning throat distracted her from her other scrapes and the inventory she was taking of all her wounds. She shook her head in disappointment with herself. It was a stupid decision, and it had been too late by the time she got there. Now she was too exhausted to leave.

It must have been hours later, because the sun was just about to dip below the horizon, which displayed a beautiful painting in the sky. She believed she had the best seat in the world for such a beautiful array of colors. She realized that at the end of every day there could be something as amazing as the sunset to look forward to; even if there is pain and sorrow, the day still ends.

Jessa was not looking forward to the long climb back down the boulders, but she knew it was going to get dark quickly. She felt an urgency to make sure Tristan was not one of the unfortunate people. She was hoping he was on the island. There was a part of her that was confident he was okay but she had no proof. She stood and turned toward the way that she had come up; she was startled to find the killer whale still down there.

She took the bamboo stick out from where she had it strapped it, took a deep breath, and jumped. There was no point in trying to climb down when she could just take a big leap. She cleared the boulders, and a rush of adrenaline went through her as she felt the work of gravity pull her to the water. The water was the perfect temperature and felt great the moment her body was enveloped into it. She had to swim for a while to get to the top.

Jessa began to stroke back towards the island when the killer whale came up alongside her. She grabbed onto one of the fins without even thinking, as if it was an automatic part of her and the whale. All at once, they took off towards the island and she was brought as close to shore as possible.

"Thank you," she whispered to the whale and patted her as she swam the rest of the way to the beach. The waves grew a little bigger as she got closer to shore; a couple took her under for longer than she preferred. By the time she was able to walk up the rest of the way, she was so weak she decided to crawl as the waves still came over her. She had to put her bamboo stick where she had strapped it to her back to make it onto the sandy beach.

Jessa sat at the waterline for a moment as she rested and caught her breath. She didn't think it was possible to swallow so much saltwater and still survive. She knew she was dehydrated, crabby, and tired. Light was fading fast, and she had to find out if Tristan was okay and find a place to sleep and build a fire. She got up on shaky legs and wobbled towards the palm trees.

A voice stopped her.

"Have you lost your mind?" Tristan yelled.

Jessa shrunk back from the anger in his voice. "I know; I'm sorry. I should have waited to get more training."

Tristan stopped right in front of her, eyes blazing. "So that was your death wish, to get ripped to shreds by the creature?"

"No! I wanted to help." Jessa felt her anger rise.

"That is not your problem. Remember you wanted to leave?" Tristan threw her previous argument in her face.

"You heard the screams. Those people!" Jessa gestured toward the boulders.

"Again, not your problem," Tristan stared at her.

"That's not fair," Jessa said, forcing herself not to cry.

"You should have listened to me. Instead I come back here to find you gone. Any idea how that felt for me?" Tristan said.

"I'm sorry. I can't just stay here when—" Jessa tried to explain.

Tristan interrupted: "I don't understand you."

"What do you mean?"

"Why do you care?" Tristan asked, tilting his head to the side.

"I..." She paused, trying to think of how to explain. "It's just the way I've always been."

Tristan started walking off.

"Where are you going?" Jessa called after him, shivering a little as the cool breeze picked up.

"I need a moment," Tristan said over his shoulder.

Jessa shook her head and continued to walk up to the palm trees, agitated by the argument. It seemed like things were finally getting comfortable with him and then she made him angry again. The words they spoke to each other played over in her mind. Her actions were, as usual, hasty and not thought all the way through. It was a life struggle for her. She sighed in frustration. Looking around for a place to set up for the night. Over the last hour of failed attempts to get a fire started she was caught off guard when she heard a voice.

"So, looks like you have met her."

Jessa stiffened and turned towards the voice and saw Tristan sitting comfortably against a palm tree. "Met who?"

"Your killer whale," Tristan answered, trying to keep the irritation from his voice.

"That's my killer whale?" she asked as she pointed out to the ocean.

"Yup," he said.

"How long have you been sitting there?" Jessa asked.

"A while…I needed to get some space," Tristan said.

"And before you came up to yell at me, how long were you waiting?"

"I'm not sure. Quite some time, probably. After we cleaned up and informed families of their losses I came quickly to check on you," Tristan shrugged.

"So you just sat there while I rolled around in the water and struggled up the shore!" Jessa yelled.

"Yup," Tristan said.

"That's some protecting skills you have, Tristan. Is that what you were talking about when you said you were my 'protector'? Because you don't have to worry about coming with me then when I go to the ship; I am sure I can do the same exact thing without an audience," she yelled.

Tristan waited only a moment before saying, "I assumed that if you had the skills and training necessary to take down the creature you would be able to swim to shore too. I mean, that is why you risked your life out there, right, because you knew exactly how to kill that thing."

Jessa took a few steps back. "No, I—"

"That's what I thought, but what could I know. Wanting you to stay here where it is safer was too much to ask, huh?" he interrupted.

"Tristan, you're right." Jessa gave up. It wasn't worth fighting about and honestly, he was right.

Tristan opened his mouth to continue to argue but stopped and stared at her. He dragged a hand through his hair and sighed. He couldn't believe how scared he was when he found the beach deserted. The fear shot through him so fast, and he didn't want to experience that again. If he hadn't seen her sitting for hours on top of the boulder, he would have lost his mind, instead he just watched her. He recalled thinking that he would have his hands full with the little warrior.

While he was thinking, he noticed she was gathering palm tree fronds. He tried to pull himself together; he didn't want to go for another walk to cool off. He had never been so distracted by a female before in his life. His heart was all tied up and his stomach clenched—feelings he was not familiar with and wasn't too fond of. He brushed them off and tried to find a lighter topic to distract himself.

"What are you going to name your whale?" Tristan asked.

"What are you talking about?" Jessa asked, clearly distracted by her task.

"I asked what you were going to name your killer whale," Tristan said.

"You know, I was actually worried about you. I cannot believe I wasted my time," Jessa said; she wasn't done with the argument. She took her bamboo stick out and jabbed it into the sand.

"It looks like you are setting up camp here. Is there a reason you don't want to sleep at my home?" Tristan said behind her as she arranged the leaves.

"A big reason would be that I don't really like you right now. The second reason is that I am way too tired to go all the way into that rainforest. If you hadn't noticed, I had to swim all the way to the boulders and it was no easy task," Jessa answered.

"You know, for someone that was so worried about me, it took you a long time to come back to the island," Tristan said, trying to keep a handle on his emotions.

"I wasn't going to stand around here on the beach, hearing people scream, and do nothing. Although by the time I got there, the damage had been done and there really wasn't anything I could do anyway," she said.

"There were only five deaths, and most of them were new people that had not been mated yet. For some weird reason, the wounded people were completely healed before we even brought them to shore," Tristan said.

"Well, I am happy for them, but those five people are dead. No matter where a person is from, a death like that is not good." Jessa gritted her teeth.

"You are right. It's just…we've had worse," he said.

"Listen, Tristan, I'm tired…just go away," Jessa said.

"As you wish. Be careful; the night brings the worst type of animals," Tristan said with a smile as he left her there. He was irritated enough not to try and argue the reasons he should stay.

"Thanks for the warning—it's nice to actually get one before the fact," Jessa muttered to herself as she settled into her bed of leaves. She was hoping that the leaves would keep some warmth, but they didn't provide very much and the sand underneath her had already begun to cool. She was tired enough not to let that bother her too much, but she already missed the comfort of a soft bed.

Once she was able to finally relax, a loud, piercing sound startled her and she instantly sat up. Her heart was racing, and she began to sweat against the chilly air. She looked around and was unable to find where the sound was coming from. She grabbed her bamboo stick and pulled it close to her chest. Her eyes were darting around the darkness, looking for something or someone that would make that sound.

A crunch of leaves behind her caught her attention; she jumped up with her bamboo stick poised up in the air ready to strike whatever it was that made the sound. After standing there for several long minutes, she began to feel her muscles shake from already being too tired. The only sounds were the crashing ocean waves and the creatures in the rainforest; the sound of crunching leaves was gone. She slowly sat back down on her blanket of leaves. She took a deep breath and let it out slowly, and she continued to breathe deliberately until she fell into a deep sleep.

Chapter 8

Teagan wrapped her arms tightly around herself as if to hug in everything that she was feeling—the terror and cold of being left alone on the ship. It hadn't been long since she saw her parents jump off the ship with the Thornbergs when the captain announced Valley Land.

The wind picked up and whirled around her. She gritted her teeth as she felt Anita hovering around her. More than once she had yelled at her, thinking she was an incompetent girl. She wanted an explanation and it wasn't as if she didn't try after Micah jumped over the edge of the ship. Talking to the captain was a loss, because he was not available at the moment. She had bloodied her hands trying to get him to open the door.

Teagan shook her head as she looked at the deck of the ship. It was littered with luggage that no one had taken with them. Not a single person was on the deck of the ship except her and Anita. The rest of the crew must've gone below. There was a hollowness in the air, and her chest ached with a pain she'd never felt before. She reasoned several times that it was just a dream and at some point she would wake up.

"Miss Robinson, is there anything I can get you?" Anita asked in a sweet voice.

Teagan whipped around. "Mind bringing my family back?"

Anita didn't get a chance to answer because the captain came over the intercom and announced the last spot on the journey: "Mythical Land."

Teagan looked around and couldn't help but laugh, as there was no one left on the ship to jump over the ledge. She laughed hard and couldn't stop until she had tears streaming down her face.

"So what are you going to do with me? Since I refuse to jump over the ledge of this stupid ship, are you going to bring me back to The Depot and unload me like a piece of luggage?" Teagan asked.

There wasn't a sound, and Teagan turned and found that Anita had disappeared. Now she truly was alone on the deck of the wooden ship. Her legs couldn't hold her up anymore and she fell right on the deck. She struggled to pull in air to breathe. Eventually, she noticed the luggage spattered on the deck blur and then everything went black.

Jessa woke up to a tickling feeling on her arm and the sun caressing her cheeks. It was a warm feeling until she opened her eyes and saw a giant tarantula crawling down her arm. She yelped and jumped up, brushing furiously at her body, making sure that there was no other chance of mystery creatures. She noticed she had some bug bites along her legs. They itched, so she walked towards the water, frustrated with the entire situation. She was supposed to wake up in her own comfy bed, no bug bites, no tarantulas, and no scary creatures.

Hoping that the water would soothe the itchy feeling the bug bites left behind, she sat in the shallow part of the water; the warm water lapped up her legs. It wasn't until she was sitting in the water that she noticed how stiff her muscles were. She didn't know whether to attribute that to her crazy excursion to the boulders or her tense muscles throughout the night. On several occasions, she had woken to unexplainable sounds.

"So much for the unbelievable paradise," Jessa complained to herself. She couldn't help but remember how delighted she was at seeing the perfect land, and how it pulled her from everything that was explainable and comfortable. She looked out at the glittering water and noticed a long, black fin come up.

On impulse, she got up and waded out deeper into the water. When she got deep enough, she dove under and swam towards the spot where she last saw the fin. Under the water, she saw the beautiful creature swimming around, doing somersaults and flips right in front of her. Then the killer whale swam up to her and nudged her with her snout. Jessa floated up to the surface and started giggling as the killer whale began to show off in front of her.

She stroked the rubbery skin on the killer whale and said, "So you are mine, huh."

"You're lucky that is a female killer whale. She will provide many protectors for you, until they are joined with their human," Tristan's voice sounded over the water.

Jessa looked over and saw Tristan with Niko; he was

smiling brightly at her as if he hadn't ditched to the wiles of the evil night. She glared at him for a moment, but wasn't able to hold it as the killer whale nudged her.

"So did you name her yet?" Tristan asked.

"Not yet." Jessa looked at the animal that was supposedly hers.

"It's a very big deal here. Culturally, it's giving someone the finishing touches to their identity. Your killer whale there will feel complete with a name," Tristan responded.

"Interesting. What are the 'finishing touches' to your identity?" Jessa asked with a smirk.

"I wish it were as simple as a name," Tristan said with an innocent smile.

"So, what makes you feel complete then?" Jessa pushed further.

"It doesn't matter," Tristan shrugged.

"Naoki. That's her name," Jessa said as she turned back to her killer whale and kissed her snout. Naoki did flips and splashed with her fluke. Niko went to join Naoki with flips and splashing around Tristan and Jessa.

"That's a good name," Tristan said quietly.

"It reminds me of a place I volunteered at. There was a white beluga whale with that name." Jessa was beginning to feel uncomfortable under his stare as she was treading water next to him.

"So how did you sleep last night, Warrior Woman?" Tristan asked with a chuckle.

"Like crap...'Warrior Woman,' what's that about?" Jessa asked.

"I think it is a great descriptor of the way you looked with the bamboo stick in your hand, ready to strike whatever came near you last night," Tristan said.

"You *saw* me?" Jessa yelled more than asked.

"Where do you think the sounds came from?" Tristan started laughing and swimming back towards the shore.

"You were the one making all those sounds, keeping me up all night scared out of my mind!" Jessa swam after him.

By the time they reached the beach, she was screaming mad, but she was out of breath as she tried to make her point. There were several times that she stumbled as a wave trampled her. Coughing out a little more saltwater, she tried to get her breath. She gripped the sand with her hands as if it could be used as a weapon, and then released, trying to regain control of her temper.

"That was the meanest and coldest...what kind of person would do that!" she finally choked out. She gripped her bamboo stick, giving up hope of reigning her temper in.

"My favorite part was the tarantula bit," Tristan said as he dodged her bamboo stick.

"Tell me you did not put that huge spider on my arm!" Jessa yelled at him.

"Whatever you want to hear," he said with a big smile.

Jessa started chasing him down the beach, throwing stones with all the power she had, and missing only a couple of times. Their quick footsteps kicked up and tossed sand into the air. The breeze was little help in keeping them cool on this warm morning. Tristan whirled around when one hit him in the head, and the chase reversed with her screaming. She couldn't help but start laughing. She was still giggling as she felt his hands grip her waist and pull her down in the sand.

"I think we need to start over"" Tristan said, bringing the mood down immediately.

"I rather like having reasons to not like you, and the huge spider was a perfect excuse," she responded.

"As fun as it is to be disliked, I prefer not to be disliked by you," Tristan explained.

"I suppose a new start would be good. Just be patient with me, please," Jessa reasoned.

"I will try. Please give this place a chance, and give me a chance," Tristan replied.

"Well, I haven't left yet. Obviously I woke up on an island, instead of in my own comfortable bed. I have bug bites to prove it," Jessa said.

"You don't need to prove anything to me; I was next to you all night…" Tristan said as he moved a piece of her hair behind her ear.

"You were? Aside from trying to scare me all night?" Jessa asked as she reached up to her hair, knowing it would be unmanageable.

"I have to make sure you are okay at all times," Tristan said.

Jessa got up, getting uncomfortable again. "Well, as you said, I am 'Warrior Woman.' I can take care of myself. I just need to get used to my surroundings a little bit more and learn some skills here."

"So you are staying?!" Tristan jumped up.

"I still think I should find my family soon. I am worried about them, but that doesn't mean I will never come back. Hey, if each of my family members are at a different Land, does that mean my parents split up?" Jessa asked.

"No, they are a pair and they are meant to stay together. They will find a land that will speak to them both equally," Tristan answered.

"Okay, that's good." She sighed.

"Want to meet my family?" Tristan asked.

Jessa looked down at her sarong and swimsuit. "Is there a place where I can wash up?" She imagined she didn't smell too pleasant either.

Tristan jumped up and held his hand out for her. They walked back to the tree line and back into the rainforest. Jessa was starting to imagine being able to navigate the rainforest by herself one day. She did not like to be dependent on anyone; it was something she always disliked. As she was thinking about this, something pierced the bottom of her foot. It was an immense pain she hadn't felt before, as if stepping on a nail. It felt like it went all the way through.

"Ouch!" Jessa cried out as she grabbed for her foot.

Tristan was instantly at her side, kneeling over her foot. She sat down on a fallen tree with his help and looked down at the trickling blood. A small puncture wound marked the place where something sharp had pierced her. Jessa could not keep the tears from forming in her eyes, it hurt so badly. She was grateful that blood did not make her stomach weak.

"That hurts really badly. Why does it sting so much?" Jessa was surprised by the amount of pain for such a small wound.

Tristan looked around for what she stepped on and then answered, "I need to make you some shoes soon. You stepped on a poisonous thorn. This isn't good Jessa; I have to get you to my family's home quick, so they can try to get to the poison before it does too much damage." Tristan was starting to panic.

"It really hurts; it feels like something is crawling under my skin up my leg!" Jessa's panic was matching his. Tristan was just about to lean over and try to suck the poison out when she bumped his head with the same thought. She could barely see through the tears as she bent over her foot. Several of her tears dripped down onto the wound as she tried to get a better look at the damage. In only a few moments, she felt instant relief and sagged back against the tree. She was secretly thankful for the way this place had quicker healing, because she hadn't wanted to put her mouth to her foot.

"That feels so much better," Jessa said with a sigh.

"Jessa?" Tristan questioned.

"Huh?" Jessa barely uttered.

"How did you do that?" Tristan asked.

"How did I do what?" Jessa started to sit up.

"Your foot…it looks as if nothing happened," Tristan said in wonder.

"Isn't that what happens here? The healing process—doesn't it speed up or something?" Jessa asked.

"No. We are susceptible to the same healing process as you. The Lands may seem magical but we have the same... Unless..." Tristan trailed off in bewilderment.

"I thought…" Jessa wasn't able to finish what she said as she stared at her hands and then her foot. Then she looked right into Tristan's eyes as the pieces to the puzzle came together for her. "Holy crap…you mean to tell me that…that I'm doing this?" Jessa asked cautiously.

"I've never seen that before in my life, if that's what you are getting at," Tristan said.

"How am I doing that?" Jessa asked.

"I have an idea. We can try it out if you want. I need you to cry for me again," Tristan said.

"Well, it's not like I can just push them out on command," Jessa said, and realized that he was thinking the same thing as her. It would explain what happened back at the boulders when her tears hit the water—Tristan said the wounded were healed before they reached shore—and also when her hands healed after they touched her face, but not her knees.

She concentrated on crying, trying to think about things that could make her sad, but she was coming up dry. Then Tristan said something. "Think about your family and the fact that you won't see them ever again."

"*What?!*" She said, and instantly the thought brought tears to her eyes. Tristan caught a tear gently with his finger before it dropped down her cheek and ran his finger along her leg where the bug bites were. Jessa lost track of what had caused the tears as her focus shifted to the tenderness of his touch on her leg. She was transfixed by the movement of his finger as he trailed her tear down it. Each bug bite healed up right before her. Her eyes grew large as she watched. After a short time, all of her wounds were completely healed.

"Were you telling the truth, that I would never see my family again?" Jessa choked out, tears brimming in her eyes again.

"No, you can see them whenever you want," Tristan answered and then continued, "But it worked. I can't believe it! You are a healer! My mate is a healer!"

"Now just a minute, I don't like the idea that I have to cry to heal someone," Jessa argued.

"Do you realize how many lives you could save with your ability? We have very limited resources for healing ointments. We don't have any that work that fast." Tristan's eyes were sparkling with wonder.

"Weren't we on our way to a place to clean up?" Jessa shifting uncomfortably, the attention was unsettling.

"Yes, we were." He held out his hand and they walked for another ten minutes before they reached huge waterfall that fed a clear lake. Jessa could almost see to the bottom.

"If you want to disrobe and hand the clothing to me, I can clean that while you wash up," Tristan offered.

"I can clean them when I get out there. Do you have any soap?" Jessa asked.

"I can make some real quick," Tristan said.

Tristan hopped off into the forest and was gone for about five minutes before he came back with a thick, liquid substance in his hands. He looked at it with pride and extended his hands. "Here you go. Do you need me to go out there and help you?"

"Ah, no. Thank you for making this. It smells good, too!" Jessa tried to sound very appreciative; it was sweet of him.

"I mixed a flower in with it." Tristan grinned.

Jessa took off her sarong since she had her swimsuit on underneath.

"I can wash that for you," Tristan offered.

"Okay. That would be great." Jessa realized he was just trying to be extra helpful—which was a massive change from a few hours ago, when he was making sounds in the forest to scare her.

She put her feet in the water; the water was much colder than the ocean. She took some of the liquid from Tristan and waded out to the waterfall. She was careful to not get caught too far under it, because she didn't want to get sucked under. She was conservative with the soap at first—wanting to make sure she got everywhere she needed to. The floral scent surrounded her, and she felt a great calm as she cleaned herself up.

She gripped the strings on her swimsuit and with a tug the top came off and then she shimmied out of her bottoms and made sure to use the remaining soap to clean her swimsuit thoroughly. She used the waterfall to rinse off; she had to use the rock ledge as leverage. She found a spot that she could sit on along the ledge so she was nestled behind the waterfall. Jessa opened her mouth to allow some water down her throat—she had forgotten how thirsty she was until that moment. She discretely put her swimsuit back on after a moment and then swam back to where Tristan was still fervently washing her sarong.

"I think you may have rolled around in the mud." Tristan chuckled as he tried to scrub some of the muddy stains out.

"Yeah, that's possible," she answered casually, feeling

much better and refreshed.

"There is blood on here... Yours?" Tristan's concerned was etched on his face.

"Of course; did you not witness how clumsy I am here? I also climbed a wall of boulders yesterday...that got messy. That's when I met Naoki," Jessa said.

"Naoki is mated to Niko now—isn't that awesome?" His facial expression sobered when he continued, "But if you leave, she will be without you to protect and will not know what to do." Tristan's tone was pleading.

"It's weird how connected I feel to Naoki already; I don't want to leave her," she said and thought to herself: *I don't want to leave you, either.*

"So, did you think you could fight the creature?" Tristan asked with a hint of a smile, wanting to keep conversation going.

"Yeah. Well, you thought you could," Jessa responded.

"Why do you think the creature left so quickly? I did fight, and won," Tristan said with pride.

"I don't mean to rain on your parade, Tristan, but if

you had won, the creature would be dead and five people's lives would have been spared. We lost." Jessa said.

"You lost nothing." Tristan said angrily and got up from washing the sarong and threw it at her.

"I'm sorry, I shouldn't have said that. You are right," Jessa said.

Tristan paced on the edge of the trees that lined up around the crystal clear lake. He shoved his hands through his hair, trying to get his irritation under control. He wondered why she sparked so many emotions within him so quickly. His control was unraveling.

Jessa watched him closely as she put her sarong back on. His pacing was unnerving. *Why did I say that?* she wondered. Everything was going so well and then she had to say something to make it bad. She wanted him happy and chastised herself for being the reason he wasn't. She was always saying and doing things without thinking. Here was another prime example of why she needed to change that behavior.

She took a deep breath and walked over to him, standing right in front of him and forcing him to abruptly stop. She stared at him, looking deeply in his blue eyes. They didn't say anything for a long time, but just looked at each other. Jessa reached up and gently rested her hand on his cheek; it wasn't smooth, indicating that he hadn't gotten a chance to shave in a few days.

"I really am sorry. Please forgive me." Jessa's breath caught in her throat at the contact.

Tristan took a deep breath and closed his eyes to try to break the connection passing between their eyes. She was hard to read, and the frustration was boiling over in him. But when she was right in front of him with those eyes—those big brown eyes—with thick, dark lashes that matched the color of her long, thick, brown hair. At times he could see red colors reflecting in her hair. This was the first time she'd touched him. He appreciated the distraction from his present feelings, but it only got him to think about another problem—he longed for her to want him more than just a mate.

He caught her wrist in his strong hand; his touch was like fire. His grip was sure and tight, yet gentle at the same time. Jessa jolted at the fierceness in his eyes when he finally opened them. She swallowed and felt her heartbeat pick up. She watched as his eyes looked at her face and her hair and wondered what he was thinking.

Tristan cleared his throat. "We should get going."

Jessa blinked in response and nodded, struggling to find her voice.

Anita's voice came through the quiet that Teagan had been in. A splash of water to the face woke Teagan up completely. She was wiping the water out of her eyes when Anita spoke in a soft whisper.

"The captain would like to see you."

"It's about time. What happened to me?" she asked.

"Miss Robinson, you fainted. You have been through a lot today, and you haven't found your place yet," Anita answered with a bit of confusion.

"I figured that out on my own, thanks," Teagan said, and pulled herself up.

She followed Anita down the wood-planked deck. She shivered a little as a cold breeze pulled her hair around. This time she left her luggage behind. They went up the small staircase and knocked on the door Teagan had previously left her DNA stamp on from knocking so hard. The door opened slowly, and Anita gestured for Teagan to enter.

The room was dark—too dark to see around it. A small candle was flickering on top of a wooden table. The curtains must have been pulled over the windows to make the room so dark, but Teagan had no way of knowing for sure. She stood just inside the door when Anita pulled it shut and left her alone in the room.

It was so quiet that Teagan could hear her own breathing. Soon she felt her heartbeat race and could barely focus on anything but the fact that she felt even more alone in the captain's quarters than on the deck. She went over the different questions that needed to be asked. Her palms were starting to sweat. After a moment, she was beginning to think there was no one else in the room.

"So you are the one that has been left behind?" a deep voice said from the other side of the room.

Teagan recognized the voice from the intercom. "It appears that way."

"It has been a long time since I have seen this," the voice said.

"So this has happened before?" she asked.

After a long pause the captain responded, "Only once."

"Well, at least it has happened before. How long has

this stupid ride been going on?" Teagan couldn't keep her impatience from creeping into her voice.

"I had to make a whole new land just for the last time...I can't believe..." The captain seemed to be talking to himself, which frustrated Teagan even more.

"Hello, I'm still here!" she yelled.

"Oh, yes. Sorry about that," the captain said. He had finally come out of one of the dark corners of the room.

Teagan was shocked by what she was looking at. The captain was a very imposing figure—his size was remarkable. He wasn't just abnormally tall, he was also proportionally large in build. His hands would not only eclipse her own but could easily palm a large watermelon—at least, that is what it looked like to Teagan from her vantage point. He had dark, gray eyes that pierced through her as he looked directly into her eyes from where he was standing. The captain had a nicely trimmed beard, and he didn't look as old as he sounded.

He stared at her for the longest time before he continued. "This 'ride', as you like to think it is, has been 'going on' for as long as humans have been around, or thereabouts."

Teagan felt a little lightheaded, thinking that it was a

lot shorter than that. "So, what happened to the last person that was left?" She gulped and continued, "Did that person go to Hell? Is that the other Land you created?"

The captain just chuckled for a moment.

"This isn't funny! To be completely honest, this whole trip has felt like Hell, so if there is another one that I am 'destined' to be at, I'd rather just go back home," Teagan argued.

That sobered the captain up. "That is your choice, of course. If you do choose to leave the Lands, you will never see your family again. However, I do have a Land that was specifically prepared for you. It is called Oracle."

"I haven't heard you announce Oracle, though, have we not reached it?" Teagan asked.

"That Land has only been occupied once. I would just take you there. As you are the only one left, there's no need for announcing it," he answered.

Teagan rubbed her head. "I'm confused. This doesn't sound like good news. My family is gone, I'm left here with you...I hate this vacation! When am I going to wake up?"

"Perhaps you would like to visit a family member.

This might make you feel better about staying here in the Lands. After that, I will take you to Oracle," the captain tried to reason.

Chapter 9

Tristan and Jessa were still trudging through the rainforest when he finally broke through the sound of loud birds, insects, and other animals. "There will be people still in mourning over the lost lives."

"I thought you said they were new; why would they have family mourning them?" Jessa asked.

"It's tradition to mourn those lost. I am positive there are those that mourn a lost life in some way," Tristan reasoned.

They neared the outskirts of what appeared to be a little village. Their homes were made out of several different materials. As they walked down the path warn down in between homes, Jessa marveled at the abilities the native people had in building them. One person had hollowed out the biggest tree she had ever seen and used that as a home. Another had used the hide of a very large animal; it looked similar to a tee-pee. Others had used trees and made log homes. The one that made her stop in her tracks was made of a skin that she had never seen before; it was pitch black and had a snakeskin texture to it. It sent shivers down her spine.

"That was made of one of the creatures we were able to kill," Tristan explained.

Jessa was in shock. She didn't know the creature could be killed, and she didn't know there was more than one. She was pulled along again, past several more unique houses. Every once in a while, Tristan would explain where the shoemaker lived, and where the glassblower, leather maker, and their own little bakery were. Tristan explained that these were all individuals with talents before they came to the Land, and they contributed their skills to help the village. Seeing families together and children running around made her think about her own family. It had only been a little over a day, but it felt like much longer.

Jessa could tell they were nearing his own family's home as she saw homes come into view. She pulled him back for a moment. "Wait, how do I look? I mean, I don't have a mirror or a way to do my hair…it just doesn't feel right showing up looking like a jungle girl."

Tristan chuckled. "I think you look amazing, but if you are concerned I can do something with your hair."

"I am concerned," Jessa said, curious what he could do with her hair.

"Okay, hold on. I have to make a stop at the leather shop," Tristan said and left her there in the dirt walkway.

A few moments later, he came back, took her hand, and brought her over to a log that was used as a bench and had her sit down. He stood behind her and began to run his fingers through her hair. At first it was a little difficult, with all the snarls, but after a while he was able to smooth her hair out. She had never been one to enjoy other people messing with her hair, but this felt amazing. He twisted it around and maneuvered strands of hair around. She could feel her shoulders relax at his touch, and she closed her eyes for a moment. When he was finished, she felt a long, thick braid down her back, with strands of leather woven through and a piece of leather tying it off at the end. It felt perfectly done, as if he'd had practice.

"There, Warrior Woman, your hair should no longer be a concern," Tristan said.

"Thank you very much," she said as she felt the braid. She was awed by the talents he possessed. He got up and began walking down the narrow path again.

She followed Tristan until they stopped at one of the larger homes, built out of logs. Jessa was not able to spend much time admiring the work done on the home before a woman tumbled out of the doorway and grabbed her in a big bear hug.

"Oh, wow, I was wondering when we would get to meet you!" the woman exclaimed.

"Mother, this is Jessa," Tristan said with a mild annoyance at his mother's inability to contain her excitement.

Three more individuals trickled out of the house and stared at her as if she were an alien; but then, that could be the truth—she wasn't exactly from this place. The father introduced himself in a less overbearing way, with a handshake and his name, Jonah. The other two came forward at the urging of the parents; Tristan's younger brother, Royce, and the youngest—a little girl, Omni. Jessa thought Omni was adorable, and Royce had some similar characteristics to Tristan. Royce was only a little younger than Tristan, and Omni looked as if she was ten years old. The mother's name was Grace, and she was easy to care for with her sweetness.

"It's nice to meet you Mrs. —" Jessa held her hand out.

"Oh, please call me Grace," she interrupted and grabbed her hand to pull her in for another hug. "I am so excited to meet you!"

Jessa just smiled, not knowing how to respond to the joyful woman. Grace gestured for them to go inside the house. The tour of the house did not take long, as it was only one bedroom and a loft. Grace explained that the house was really only a place to lie down, as most of the family was busy outside of the house. Omni was jumping around, distracting Jessa from Grace's talk about village life. After a moment, Royce, Jonah, Omni, and Tristan left to take care of some household chores and the house got noticeably quiet.

Jessa sat down at the table after Grace's strong urging. Grace began to fill a pot of water for some tea, and then turned to pull down a tin full of biscuits. Grace continued chattering away; Jessa could hardly keep up but found herself quickly becoming very fond of the woman. She had a glow about her that was warm and comforting. Jessa caught herself smiling at the woman. When Grace finally took a breath, Jessa used it as her opportunity to start asking questions.

"So, tell me about Tristan—I haven't gotten a chance to know him that well." Jessa blushed at her own forwardness.

"Oh, heavens! Where do I start?" Grace paused for a moment before launching into his birth and little habits he had as a child. Grace started talking about his first time at the beach and how he wasn't allowed to touch the water until a certain age, when Jessa interrupted.

"Is it a rule, people can't touch the water until they are older? Is there a specific age?"

"Well, not so much a rule, but a strong recommendation. Since there are so many things that happen when a person touches the water, they should stay out of the ocean until they are ready and old enough to mate. Time works a little bit differently here, as I'm sure you have noticed. But since I am from earth too, I will try to talk in the same timeframe as you are familiar with. At about age 17, they can go to the ocean if they wish; so many are so eager that they leave for the ocean right as they turn that age. Our eldest son waited much longer than most we have seen. He is 21 years old, but really he is much older than that in this land," Grace interrupted her own explanation.

"When will Royce be old enough?" Jessa was trying to get a grasp on his age.

"He already is old enough, but he has been so busy lately with training and hasn't gone," Grace answered.

"He looks a lot like his brother. I wish I knew Tristan better; it's been a little difficult," Jessa answered quietly.

"Oh, well, there is plenty of time for that. Are you pleased with him?" She patted Jessa's knee, not worried at all of how awkward the question was.

Jessa felt her face flame hot, and she looked down at the tea cup Grace set down in front of her. "I..." She looked up and saw such an expectant look in Grace's face that she just said, "Yes."

Jessa offered a small smile after that, realizing that she could be pleased with him if she just gave him a chance. If she had been more understanding of the position she was putting him in by wanting to leave, she wondered if she would have seen a different side of Tristan. She recalled seeing a glimpse of the real Tristan just before she started talking about going back to the ship. He looked so happy, as if his life had just started.

After a period of silence, Jessa shook the thoughts loose and sighed. "I have so many questions—I really don't even know where to start. Can I do the training you mentioned Royce was doing?"

"Tristan is supposed to teach you survival skills," Grace answered.

"Okay, so Royce is learning survival skills? Let's pretend he doesn't teach me, where do I get the lessons?" Jessa pushed.

"Royce has already acquired all of his survival skills training. Now he is doing his last sessions on combat training. Why wouldn't Tristan teach you?" Grace looked concerned.

"What if I wanted to learn more than just survival? What if I wanted to learn more about the combat training?" Jessa avoided Grace's question.

Grace looked bothered by the question. "That is something that is taught to the males in the village, not the females, since the males are considered the protectors along with the killer whales. Have you met yours yet?" Grace's eyes lit up.

"Yes, I have. Her name is Naoki," Jessa answered, a little disappointed in what Grace was saying.

"That's a beautiful name; you have a talent for names," Grace said, unable to hide her excitement.

"Names are not the only gift she has, Momma," Tristan interrupted. Jessa did not know how long he had been listening.

"Oh, yeah, do tell please, Tristan." Grace looked at her son with adoration.

"She is a healer," Tristan said with pride.

"What? You must be joking. I haven't even seen a healer in this Land. I have only heard of them, and they stay at Beneath Land for preservation and as royalty." Grace looked worried.

"Would they do that?" Tristan sat down next to Jessa with concern.

"It's possible," Grace said showing no emotion.

"I won't allow it!" Tristan pounded his fist on the table, making Jessa and Grace jump.

"You may not have a choice, Tristan. If she chooses to go or if the Oracle requests her, then she is free to go," Grace said.

"No, I forbid it!" Tristan yelled.

"What is going on? You cannot talk to your mother like that, young man," Jonah cut in from the front doorway.

"I'm sorry," Tristan said as he got up and left the house.

Grace and Jessa looked at the door Tristan just left through, and both of them looked a little upset by what happened. Jessa couldn't help but wonder about Beneath Land; it seemed like an enigma. She wondered how many people were being 'preserved' there. It was like Oracle Land, where there wasn't much information given in the title, just more questions. She wanted to ask about both of those Lands, but decided to save it for another time.

"Excuse me. Perhaps we can talk some more later. Like I said, I have so many questions," Jessa said as she left out the front door.

"Of course, my dear…I would love to see you again, and soon!" Grace called out after her.

"Tristan! Hold up. What is going on?" Jessa grabbed his arm to turn him around, but his muscles bunched and he pulled his arm easily from her grasp.

"I need to be alone," Tristan said.

"Okay; where do you suggest I go while you run off?" Jessa asked.

"I didn't even think about the possibility that the captain would want to take you to Beneath Land to preserve your ability. Heck, maybe you would prefer to be among the royalty," Tristan said angrily, ignoring her question.

"Well, your mother said it would be my choice. What good would it do if I was there when I could help people here?" Jessa said.

Tristan whirled around on her and pinned her with a stare. "You would choose to stay here?"

"I'll make you a deal; this will be my home on one condition. You teach me not just survival skills but the skills of a fighter—combat fighting," Jessa stated.

"You will have to think of something else," Tristan answered.

"I will learn to fight. You decide whether or not you want it to be you that teach me." She stood there with arms crossed.

"So I guess you will leave then, since I cannot abide by your conditions?" Tristan asked with a stern tone.

"I don't know." Jessa's facial expression faltered.

Tristan understood that she wanted to be alone, even though just a moment ago she didn't want him to leave her. He would just be on the outskirts of the village if she wanted him near.

"I will give you some space. I will be just outside the village," Tristan said quietly.

Jessa wrestled with her thoughts. She wanted this place to be her home, but she was exhausted of the rules, warnings, and different things to worry about. Tristan had long turned and walked away, disappearing into the rainforest. She had the most difficult time figuring out the customs of the new place; growing up in America, where women could enlist in the army, she didn't understand why women were not allowed to learn to fight. When she thought about it, her request was rather absurd. She had never wanted to join the army when she had the opportunity, but now that the option was taken from her she wanted it the most. She laughed at herself. Her only desire was to be able to fend for herself if the time came.

While these thoughts were still roaming around in her mind, she looked around at the small village. It was a cute, little place. The different shops Tristan had described came to her mind, and she got up and looked through a few of the stores. The leather store was fascinating, with all the work the tanner put into each piece of material. Then she remembered the glassblower Tristan had mentioned. As soon as she walked into the small hut to see what was there, she was in awe of the talent in the art surrounding her. There were glasses of all different colors, shapes, and sizes. Some of the smaller pieces were strung up from the ceiling. A woman greeted her with a big smile and explained a few pieces and introduced herself as Sami. Sami had fiery, red hair and freckles that added character to her facial features.

Jessa talked to Sami for some time about the different pieces in the hut and where her inspiration came from. There were tiny bottles spread out at the counter; Jessa figured Sami must have been pricing them or had just finished them. It had given Jessa a great idea. She listened to Sami describe another beautiful piece; it appeared it was one of the shop owner's favorites.

"I was wondering if you ever have situations where you get hurt and it keeps you from being able to do what you love," Jessa said after looking at several more things Sami made. Jessa guessed that Sami was around her age.

"Of course; glassblowing is extremely dangerous, and on several occasions I have gotten hurt. Ha, I don't remember a week that has gone by without some accident happening," Sami answered. A puzzled look came over her face as she asked, "Why do you ask? You thinking of learning some glassblowing?"

"No, I'll leave that talent where it belongs—with you, Sami. I was just wondering if we could barter," Jessa reasoned.

"What do you mean?" Sami asked.

"Well, I was wondering if you were able to make vials, small ones—smaller than those bottles over on the counter. I would like to fill them with a certain chemical that has been known to heal wounds in less than a few seconds," Jessa said.

"A chemical? I've never heard of such a thing. Where did you find such a chemical?" Sami asked.

"I...I cannot say right now, but I will give you the first vial full to prove it...if you find that it does not work, you can keep it and the vial. I will find some other means to pay you for the labor," Jessa said cautiously.

"I already have a little vial made; let me go get it. You fill it and bring it back to me, and if I find that it works I will make as many as you want. That healing chemical could be very helpful for the village. We could barter it for other goods, too," Sami said confidently.

"That's what I was thinking," Jessa said with a smile.

Sami handed her a small vial that fit in the palm of Jessa's hand; if Jessa closed her fingers over it, no one could see it.

"Do you have a way of making vials that can hang from a necklace?" Jessa asked before she left.

"I can do just about anything with glass. That shouldn't be hard, but I want proof first," Sami answered like a true businesswoman.

"And you will," Jessa said and left with a thank you.

Chapter 10

Jessa walked back to Tristan's family's home and knocked on the door. She felt ridiculous being there after only a short time being away. Grace answered the door and smiled big. The smile disappeared when she realized Tristan wasn't anywhere in sight.

"Is everything alright?" Grace asked.

"I didn't think I would be back this soon, but I had some more questions." Jessa smirked, avoiding her question.

Grace led her to their small wooden kitchen table and began to make some tea.

"What can I help you with, Jessa?" Grace asked cautiously, deciding not to ask about the apparent discord between her son and Jessa.

"How would the captain find out about my ability? If I keep it a secret, will he still find out somehow?" Jessa asked, getting right to the point.

"It's not best to keep things from the captain. You could be banned from the Lands. Tristan would have a difficult time finding a reason to continue living if you were. I know that sounds morbid, but it is true. The Lands thrive best on those that are mated. Somehow, it is as if the Lands need the mated pairs to keep them going," Grace answered.

"But he could mate again, just like he did before," Jessa said.

"His first mating did not last long enough to even mourn, although he did for a short while. He has become so attached to you that I don't think he would allow himself to mate again," Grace said with sadness in her voice.

Jessa had a tough time believing Grace. Tristan didn't exactly show that he was 'so attached' to her.–She knew they were mated, but it seemed that was as far as it went.

"So then maybe it is best that the captain knows

about it, but that I made my choice to stay at this Land," Jessa said.

"I fear for you, Miss Jessa, because your gift has not been seen before in this Land or in several others…I hope that the captain gives you the choice, but this Land is so dangerous. He may not like the risk, and he may take you to the Oracle Land or Beneath Land for safety and, as I said, preservation," Grace answered.

"Well, there's nothing like feeling as if one doesn't have a choice," Jessa said sarcastically and continued. "If I tell the captain, he might take me from Water Land, and if I don't tell him, he might kick me out of the Lands altogether. I will never be able to see my family again. I have grown to like this place quite a bit, despite my first night here," Jessa said.

"Tristan and you will have to decide what to do. I really want you to stay here, but I don't want to risk you getting kicked out for good. At least we can visit you if you invite us," Grace said.

"Is the Oracle Land the only one that requires an invite or something?" Jessa asked.

"Yes," Grace responded.

"And what about Beneath Land? It sounds more mysterious," Jessa wondered.

"As with all the Lands, that one is very interesting. Beneath Land is where the Royalty stays. The Captain decided to have a King and Queen and several members of the court as a request from a lot of people in the Lands. Beneath Land is one of the newer Lands," Grace answered.

"Royalty? Did people get to vote or something?" Jessa's curiosity was growing.

"Yes, but from a specific group of individuals. The royalty is comprised of people who have special abilities. It is a small enough group of people. I hear rumors of other things going on in Beneath Land that are frustrating, but I'm not sure how true they are." Grace shook her head.

"What rumors?" Jessa leaned forward.

"Oh, I'm not sure if they are true." She waved it off.

Jessa sat back and watched her, deciding not to say anything. Her mind was reeling with the thought that there was another Land that had royalty there with a King, Queen, and court members. She thought it sounded more like a fairytale the more she heard. If she had to live there, it didn't sound too bad.

"I have heard they are specifically pairing people together that have abilities—like yours—without being mated, in order to genetically enhance the race with more abilities." Grace's face showed irritation.

Jessa placed her hands on the table. "Thank goodness they are just rumors, then. Could you imagine not having a choice in who you are with? Do people live there that do not have special abilities?"

"Yes, I believe people get that pull from the ship as well. They live in the other sections."

"Sections?" Jessa tilted her head to the side.

"Oh, yes. Beneath Land is an underground network of cities. You should really see it sometime; it is quite fascinating," Grace responded.

"Underground? Wow." Jessa shook her head. "Have you been to any of the other Lands?" Jessa asked.

"Oh, yes! They are all quite unique. Jonah and I decided that we wanted to visit them all at some point. Except, of course, Oracle Land. Forest Land is the first one, and we had to wait a while to see that one because on our first ship ride, we jumped into this Land right away, as does everyone when they feel the pull towards a particular Land. The ship goes back and forth between each Land in a successive line, only stopping at the Depot once a year. When you have your rope held out, you move in space and time to wherever the ship is at that time. If you jump off onto a Land and take a piece of the Land with you, then you can just jump to that Land rather than having to go onto the ship and wait. It's called a token. You would have the token from that Land and the rope, and it will whisk you away to that Land. That makes it easier to visit family when you want to. Some families make it a tradition to meet at one Land during special times or occasions." Grace told everything about the mystery Lands as if it were a story or make-believe.

"Wait, how does a person figure out the right timing if the times are different for each Land?" Jessa asked.

"The captain is very helpful with that and a lot of times families choose to meet on the ship too, because no matter what time of day or where the ship is at they can meet there and then choose a Land from there. I have seen that many times as well." Grace smiled.

"That makes sense, surprisingly," Jessa said.

"When you choose a token, you will want to make sure it is significant to that Land. A rock that can be found in more than one Land could confuse you," Grace recommended.

"Good point," Jessa said.

"Do you want to visit some other Lands?" Grace asked.

"I need to see my family. I have to make sure every-one is okay, and I would like to see what Land they chose," Jessa said.

"That is very understandable. Jonah and I were fortu-nate enough to come together on the ship and we were both pulled to this land. If we weren't, we would have had to compromise on a Land. However, it is a rare occurrence where both individuals do not feel the same pull. We did not have children at the time; in-stead we had children here. The captain really likes that; he likes to see growth in the Lands. So far, as you have seen, the children are still in this Land, but they have the choice to leave," Grace said as she poured a cup of tea. The aroma itself made Jessa's mouth water. Around that same time, the sound of her stomach growling chimed in.

"When was the last time you ate something, dear?" Grace asked.

"I ate on the ship." Jessa realized.

"Oh, heavens! Let me make you something quick to eat." Grace stood up.

"How come Tristan doesn't want to leave this Land, even just to visit another Land?" Jessa wondered aloud.

"I'm not sure; you will have to ask him. I think it

might have to do with his best friend, Cade. Cade left right after his mate died. It was a really sad story. They were mated for a long time. He left years ago and never came back," Grace answered as she set out a loaf of bread.

The bread seemed to make her stomach respond even more to the idea of food. "So, what...Tristan is afraid he will leave and not want to come back?" Jessa asked.

"Or maybe that he will leave and Cade will come back and confirm his worst fears. That he is staying away because of him," Grace said, shaking her head.

"I'm not following. Tristan thinks that if he leaves Water Land that Cade will come back while he is gone...and that is supposed to confirm that Cade is only staying away until Tristan leaves?" Jessa questioned.

"That's just a theory; like I said, you will have to ask him. There are other things that took place between Cade and Tristan, and I believe there was another girl involved...but Tristan won't talk about it," Grace said.

Jessa took a bite out of the bread as Grace brought some more food to the small table. "This is a depressing topic; let's change the subject. Tell me about yourself, Jessa. I am eager to learn more about you."

Grace eased down into a chair.

"Tell you about myself...that's a loaded statement. Where to start?" She took a breath and continued, "I grew up in Minnesota with my family. I have an older brother, Micah, and a younger sister, Teagan. We had been invited to visit the Thornberg family several times and my mother told us we all had to go. Right now it is Christmas break, so all three of us would have been home from college for the Holidays anyway. I am studying to be a marine biologist. I realized at a very young age how much I loved water life. It's kind of ironic that I am here and it is something I study in college. Micah actually has his BA and is doing some other classes; he is a bit of a techie. Teagan hasn't quite decided what she wants to do yet," Jessa said.

Grace finally took a seat at the table. "That is your family, Miss Jessa, but what about you?"

"I guess I don't really know how to answer that. No one has ever asked me that before," Jessa rolled the question over in her mind.

"What was your favorite thing to do?" Grace urged.

"Basically, anything to do with water: going to the lake, fishing, jet-skiing, you name it. Although in Minnesota there is a very small window to do that. It is commonly known that in Minnesota we have two seasons: winter and road construction—that doesn't leave a whole lot of time for water activities. While I am at college in California, I have more of an opportunity to do that, but school kind of takes over my time," Jessa tried to answer her question.

Grace laughed. "No wonder you are here in this Land."

"I have no doubt of why I am here, it's just that here nothing makes sense...this whole place is like a dream, and yet there are real dangers. Enough danger, in the water, that each person has a killer whale as a protector and a mate on land to protect as well. And now I face the danger of being put on a Land for protection, which is more like preservation. Each Land has the protectors and mates?" Jessa asked.

"Actually, yes. Each land has its dangers, so there is a protector and mate waiting for each person; unless, of course, the person is already mated, then they get a protector only," Grace answered.

"So, let's say I was pulled to Mythical Land. What kind of protector is there?" Jessa could not contain her curiosity; this Land was the one she wanted to visit the most.

"You picked the one Land that you would have the

opportunity to choose a protector, because in Mythical Land you would want to choose the protector that would be most effective against all the dangers that are there," Grace said.

"Okay, how about Forest Land?" Jessa asked.

"I believe that Land has a bear as the protector," Grace said.

"If I jumped to one of these Lands, would I get a protector and mate there?" Jessa asked.

"No; if you don't feel the pull to that Land, there is nothing waiting there for you," Grace said matter-of-factly.

"This is all just pure craziness. You know that, right?" Jessa said in frustration.

"Well, I know you aren't the first one to think that. So, did you have a boyfriend back in Minnesota?" Grace changed the subject.

"Ah, no. I dated a bit, but nothing too serious." Jessa blushed.

"Do you think there will be anyone that will notice you are gone?" Grace asked.

"I imagine relatives will eventually catch on; but you

are making it sound like this is a permanent arrangement and not a vacation," Jessa sounded concerned.

"Well, it is completely up to you if you want to leave, but I hope you decide to stay. If you leave, you can never come back. You would never be able to see your family again," Grace warned.

Jessa looked up from her empty plate of food. "I won't leave my family behind."

"I gathered that much in the time you have spent here," Grace said with a smile.

Grace got up from the table and grabbed a book from a small shelf in the corner of their home. She brought it to the table and slid it over to Jessa. "This is just in case you forget to stop by and eat here. This book shows the edible foods, both from the ocean and the island. You can keep it. It also covers mixtures for shampoos and things of that nature."

"Thank you. I suppose I'd better go, but thank you for answering some of my questions. And thank you for the delicious food," Jessa said as she left the home.

"It was my pleasure. I hope to see you soon," Grace called back.

The book Jessa had in her hand was small; she could have fit it in her back pocket if she were wearing jeans. She was leafing through some of the pages, walking down the narrow path, when Tristan fell into step with her.

"So you went to visit my mother again, huh?" he asked.

"Yes; she answered some of my questions," Jessa answered.

"I see," he said.

"So, are we good?" Jessa smiled.

"Yeah, we're good." Tristan chuckled and continued, "Did she answer all the things that I couldn't?"

"Or wouldn't?" Jessa added.

Tristan ran a hand through his hair in frustration. "You are a piece of work, you know?"

"Just because I want answers?" Jessa felt her temper rising.

"What haven't I answered?" Tristan asked, his temper starting to match hers.

"Well, for starters, you won't teach me anything," Jessa answered.

"I haven't taught you because I want to do them for you," Tristan said.

"I can't expect you to be around me all the time." Jessa stopped and looked him in the eye.

Tristan stopped. "Jessa, I can't teach you combat skills."

"I want to learn self defense. I don't want to be dependent on anyone! I have felt dependent on your every move since I jumped off that ship. I am clinging to the hope that I won't need someone the way I need you," Jessa yelled.

She knew it was going to happen—she was going to lose her control and say something she would regret. She blushed and looked away, refusing to look at him, but it was so quiet that she didn't know if he was still there. There was no movement next to her. Jessa could feel her skin heat in embarrassment at the admission of needing him. She hated to admit that; she'd never needed anyone.

"It's been a long day. We should get some shut eye,"

Tristan finally said.

"Yeah, I am tired," Jessa agreed.

Tristan knelt down. "Can you lift up your left foot, please?"

She obeyed, and he strapped some leather hide on her foot and then did the same to the other.

"A storm is rolling in. The leather should protect your feet," Tristan said and started walking in the direction of his home.

"Did you make these?" Jessa caught up to him.

He nodded in response.

"Thank you." She paused. "Where are we going?"

"Well, I figured you didn't want to get soaked, so we will be staying at my home tonight. I hope that's okay with you," Tristan answered.

"Your home? Is it warmer there?" Jessa asked, recalling how cold she was the night before on the beach.

"It tends to warm up throughout the night," Tristan said, sounding somewhat evasive.

"I hope your blankets are nicer than my leaves, because those were some pretty awesome leaves," Jessa joked as she followed behind him.

Jessa had shoved the glass vial in the band of her swimsuit, but could not find a place for the book, so she held onto it as she kept pace with Tristan. She wasn't sure how he was able to navigate the thick rainforest when darkness began to fall. It was eerily silent as they hit large leaves out of their way. The bugs buzzing in her ears were the only sounds of the rainforest. She heaved a breath as their pace picked up. He appeared to be in a hurry. A vine snapped across her face, and she was about to yell out when they came to a stop.

He crouched and moved the large leaves that covered the opening. The entire rainforest went black as the sun disappeared behind the darkest clouds Jessa had ever seen. It was difficult to see the sky at all when the trees covered most of her view, but she saw just enough to see the black clouds. Just as he was crawling down the hole, a loud crack of thunder broke out overhead.

"Better hurry or you'll get wet," Tristan urged as she tried to figure a way into the dark hole.

The next loud thunder got her to scurry as quickly as she could into the hole. She tried to look around but wasn't able to see anything until Tristan put the chain around his neck with the glowing stone. It illuminated the place again and she saw the inside of his home. She looked around to see if there was more than one bed, but there was only his. He mentioned a new addition to make more space for the two of them. The new addition seemed to just be an extra space for a little table, but there wasn't a table there yet.

"I got a kill today on my way back to the village. As soon as the butcher and leather maker are done with what they need, you will have enough to make a blanket. I will share mine until then," Tristan offered.

"Share? In the same bed?" Jessa stiffened at the thought.

"Unless you are a bed hog, I don't see any problem with it," Tristan said with a smile.

"Well, you mentioned that it gets warm in here, so maybe I won't need a blanket," Jessa said innocently and tried to settle in the new addition space.

Tristan chuckled. "It gets warmer when two bodies are close together—that's what I meant."

"You aren't suggesting that we...that we, you don't mean to say that we actually..." Jessa was unable to finish her sentence, and she was grateful for the shadows in the home because she knew a blush was creeping up her face.

"That we what, Jessa?" Tristan asked.

"You know what I mean," Jessa yelped.

"I wouldn't ask if I knew what you meant," Tristan said innocently.

"Actually, I will just freeze over here with my sarong," Jessa tried to avoid having to explain.

"You would rather freeze?" Tristan sounded completely bewildered by her behavior.

"As a matter of fact, yes," Jessa said.

Another loud crack of thunder sounded above them. "It sounds like this storm is right above our heads," Jessa said in wonder and concern.

"It probably is," Tristan said.

"Won't this place fill up with water?" Jessa asked.

"No; I have created a really good draining system," Tristan answered with a yawn as he stretched out on his bed. He put the necklace back in his pouch and the room became pitch black.

"What about bugs?" Jessa said in the dark.

"What about them?" Tristan asked.

"Well, do they like to come in here and eat you?" Jessa asked.

"I have not yet experienced being eaten by a bug that has lived to tell the tale," Tristan said with a laugh.

"So, how do you sleep knowing there might be a giant tarantula climbing up your leg?" Jessa said with a quiver.

"It isn't hard to sleep if you have grown up here. Are we going to talk all night?" Tristan responded.

Jessa wanted to see how impervious he was to bugs and the fear of them. She quietly moved around in the room, making sure to move slowly as to not make a sound. She crept closer to where she remembered his bed was. It took a while before she reached her destination and even more time to find his leg. She moved her fingers like a spider would move along his ankle and was about to move her fingers up to see if he would freak out. But he snatched up her hand and pulled her up against him, as if he had seen her clear as day, and hauled her up onto his bed.

"You are full of mischief," Tristan said.

Jessa was so close, she could feel his breath fan across her face and could tell he was smiling even though it was dark in the room. He hadn't let go of her hand yet. She held her breath at the proximity of his body. He wasn't wearing a shirt, and she could feel the muscles in his chest were solid.

"Just checking to make sure you were telling the truth about the bugs not bothering you," Jessa murmured, noting that her pulse was racing.

"Did I prove it?" Tristan asked.

"Yes, without a doubt," Jessa said, trying to get her hand out of his steel grip. She hadn't realized just how strong he was; he plucked her up so quickly it threw her off.

"Good. Now that you are here…you may as well just stay and go to sleep. And be warm," Tristan said.

"I don't think that is a good idea," Jessa said as she inched away.

"Warmth and sleep is not a good idea? What kind of world did you come from?" Tristan asked.

"I came from a world that thinks sharing a bed with someone means something special," Jessa said sharply.

"Interesting," Tristan said.

"In a lot of cases it is reserved for people that love each other. Of course, that's not with many cases anymore. However, I include myself in the first bunch and reserve sharing a bed with someone that I love," Jessa answered.

"What about the promise of sleep and warmth? Doesn't that override your reserve? It can be one of the first things about survival in a place like this. Good sleep equals being more alert, among other things," Tristan responded.

"Are you teaching me skills, Tristan?" Jessa teased.

"Survival skills, which is different from fighting skills," Tristan said back, his voice echoing in the little space.

"Got it. Will you release your death grip on my hand please?" Jessa asked.

Tristan released her hand immediately; he hadn't realized he was still holding onto it. Jessa couldn't help but rub her hand. She slowly moved back to where she guessed her sarong was.

"So you choose reserve over survival. Good to know," Tristan said mockingly.

"If that is what you want to call it, then yes...for now I will. If it gets unbearable I will move," Jessa said.

"You will only share a bed with me if your other option is unbearable? What if I don't let you share my bed, now that you have chosen otherwise?" Tristan sounded a little hurt, but Jessa couldn't be sure in the dark.

"Are you trying to pick a fight?" She laughed.

"No," Tristan said quietly.

In efforts to change the topic a little, she asked, "So, have you ever seen a mated couple in love here before?"

"I have. It's beautiful, but rare. I'm fortunate to see my parents in love, since they were before they came here," Tristan said.

"That's so sad," Jessa said.

"It's just not for everyone," Tristan said curtly.

"Obviously being mated does not mean being in love. If a person spends a lifetime here, what a waste it is to be mated and yet not in love," Jessa said as she yawned.

"Being mated includes caring about each other. That's close enough," Tristan answered shortly.

Jessa didn't respond. The thought of not getting the

chance to fall in love made her shiver; she drew the sarong closer to her body. Shortly after she fell asleep, the sound of raindrops hitting the leaves lulled her to sleep. The loud crack of thunder startled her awake only a few hours later. She realized she was stiff from being in one spot for those few hours. She rolled over and tried to fall back asleep. Even though the rain did not come into his home, it still was damp and chilly. Jessa struggled to get her muscles to relax enough to fall asleep. After trying different ways to get comfortable and warm, she decided to give up hope and just lie on her back and stare at the darkness above her.

Eventually, sleep overtook her.

Chapter 11

The next morning was difficult to wake up to. Jessa was sore in places she didn't think she could be sore in. Jessa stretched and noticed a heavy blanket move around her as it draped over her body. She was not in the original place she had started out that night. She was comfortably nestled in a bed filled with some kind of stuffing. She was so cozy that she did not want to move, but that quickly changed when she realized that she was in Tristan's bed.

She sat up quickly and scanned the room. It was still dark, but she could see better with the daylight peeking through some of the trees into the hole. She was afraid to look at the spot next to her in the bed, in case he was there. She held her breath and turned and let out her breath in a whoosh when she saw that she was by herself.

Jessa didn't have time to think of much more before Tristan came bounding down the hole and into the home.

"How did you sleep?" Tristan asked.

"It was okay. Not great," she answered.

"I figured," Tristan replied.

"Your teeth were chattering loud enough to keep me awake, so I figured you may as well have the bed and I went somewhere else to sleep," Tristan said.

"I really appreciate it. What is this bed made out of anyway? It is really comfortable," Jessa asked.

"When we make your bed, I will show you. For now, I made you a pouch to put your belongings in," Tristan said.

"You did? Wow, thank you," she said as tried to get up from the cozy bed. The air around her was colder than in the bed, so naturally she wanted to curl up and stay there longer.

"I told you I would," he said.

"This looks awesome!" she responded to the crafted pouch. It looked more feminine; it was something she could sling over her shoulder or attach to her rope.

"I just treated it to a waterproofing agent, so be careful. It needs a little more time to dry," Tristan instructed.

"Thank you, again," Jessa said.

"I suppose you would like to go to the beach and swim with Naoki," Tristan changed the subject.

"Of course! I would love to," Jessa exclaimed.

Tristan led the long way back to the beach, and Jessa tried her best to remember landmarks or anything that would be able to help her back to the little village without having to ask for Tristan's help. It didn't help that there wasn't a path from the beach to the village, but Tristan explained that the villagers want to keep the place hidden for protective purposes. Therefore, a different way was used to get to the village if at all possible. Jessa sighed inwardly at the sound of that.

Jessa still held tightly to the small book and the vial that she had gotten while Tristan worked on his home the day before. They were the only items she could call her own. When they reached the beach, the sun was bright overhead; she assumed it was close to noon. Jessa hadn't realized how much time had passed. The rainforest always seemed a little darker, which made it difficult to tell what time of day it could be.

"You taking in the scenery?" Tristan asked, wondering what she was looking at.

"I am just trying to create landmarks in my mind, so I know how to get back to your home," Jessa answered.

"I will be with you. Why would you need landmarks?" Tristan asked.

"I can't expect you to be with me every moment. I don't want to be that dependent." Jessa felt like she was repeating herself as she placed the book and vial in her pouch and put it under the huge leaves up against a palm tree. When she was done covering up her only possessions with her sarong and some leaves, she stood and turned toward the water. Then she took off at a quick run towards it. Tristan stood there for two seconds before running after her. They both entered the water with a giant splash and played around in the waves. Both were desperate to change the mood that had settled over them since they were at the village.

They spent some time body surfing and splashing each other. Then they walked the beach a little bit, picking up seashells. Most of the ones they found were broken or chipped. Jessa realized how much she wanted to find the perfect seashell that could be her token from the Land that she would probably call home. Slowly, she began to accept that this mysterious and unexplainable world was something she was a part of. She might even be needed here.

She felt more than heard Naoki off in the distance. Without hesitation, she took a sharp turn and went out into the water, swimming powerfully towards Naoki. Tristan followed.

Jessa was so excited to see Naoki; she couldn't believe that she had seen her just yesterday when it felt like so much longer. Niko was quick to follow; Tristan grabbed hold of him and they went underwater. Jessa watched in wonder as they dove deep. Naoki nudged Jessa for some attention. Jessa began rubbing her snout, when Naoki opened her giant mouth. At first Jessa was scared, thinking she made Naoki mad and for a split second she thought she was going to bite her. Instead, Naoki had something in the middle of her light, pink tongue, just sitting there. Jessa reached in Naoki's mouth, thinking that in any other circumstance it would be so dangerous. She pulled the object out and immediately tears formed in her eyes as she looked at the perfect seashell.

"Naoki, you are amazing," she whispered and kissed her right on her snout. Jessa then climbed onto Naoki's back, which was no easy task, and Naoki took her around for a fun ride toward the boulders. Jessa noticed the sound of laughter in the background again, just like she had the first day she arrived. As soon as they rounded the boulders, Jessa saw at least fifty people playing in the water where the creature had just been not too long ago.

Jessa stared in horror as people acted as if nothing had happened there. She felt anger build up in her and a strong desire to yell at the people for being so heartless. The anger turned into deep sadness, and she forced Naoki to bring her back to the beach—which Naoki did with excellent speed.

When her feet connected with the sand, she ran towards the tree where her belongings were. She fumbled around for the vial as she felt tears threatening to spill down her cheeks. Finally she was able to find it and she put the vial up to her eye to catch the tears. Surprisingly, she was able to fill it as long as she didn't try to suppress any feelings she had been experiencing. Back in Minnesota, she would suppress her feelings all the time, and very rarely would she cry. She decided that her tears were worth something here, whereas before tears did nothing—they solved none of her problems, and she ended up feeling a fool for allowing something to make her cry. She'd just barely put the vial down when Tristan called out to her.

"What are you doing up there?" Tristan asked.

"Where did you go?" Jessa shot back, making sure to the purple tears before she turned around to him.

"Niko wanted to show me some cool things at the bottom of the ocean," Tristan said with a smile. He walked up to her, dripping with water. Jessa wondered if she was ever going to get used to how good he looked.

"How can you hold your breath for that long?" Jessa asked.

"I can't; it's not that deep where he took me," Tristan answered.

He was breathing deeply as if he had run a marathon. He plopped down right where Jessa was standing. That left an open invitation for her to do the same. She slid down in the sand next to him. The warmth of the sun on the sand curled around her. As her toes played in the white sand, she remembered she had forgotten the leather shoes back at Tristan's home.

"Why are all those people playing over by the boulders again so soon after...after, well, you know?" Jessa asked.

"It's kind of a statement, defiant. Showing the creature it can't take away their ability to heal," Tristan answered as he stared off at the water.

"That makes sense. I admire their strength," Jessa answered honestly.

"So, tell me about yourself Janessa Avery Robinson," Tristan said with a smile.

"That is the second time someone said that to me. And I still don't know how to respond. How about you just ask me questions and I will answer them?" Jessa said.

"My mother must have said something similar," Tristan said.

They sat on the beach for a while longer, and Jessa answered the questions that Tristan threw at her, right down to her favorite color. All of the questions were superficial and light. It was a relief to have a light conversation without getting in an argument.

Jessa knew she would ruin the moment, but she had to ask: "Who's Cade?"

"Huh?" Tristan responded without hesitation.

"Your mother mentioned Cade yesterday," Jessa said.

"He was just a friend," Tristan answered.

"Was?" she asked.

"He left a while ago." Tristan was careful to keep his answers short.

"Ah." Jessa caught the hint that he didn't really want to discuss it at the moment.

"We should probably go and get something to eat," Tristan said after a moment of silence.

"Good idea," Jessa said.

Chapter 12

"Good afternoon, Grace!" Jessa said cheerfully.

"Hello dear," Grace responded.

Tristan came over to his mother and kissed the top of her head before he sat down at the table. Jessa sat down next to him, feeling more comfortable being closer to him. Grace took in the small gesture and couldn't help but smile. Jonah came in the doorway, looking as if he had run a marathon. Royce followed behind, looking worse. Omni came running in just shortly after with a bouquet of little wildflowers she'd picked with some friends.

"Training looked like it got the best of you Jonah,"

Grace said.

"It was brutal this morning. Royce graduated to the next level, though!" Jonah said.

"Congratulations, baby!" Grace yelled as she ran to the teenager and humiliated him with a wet kiss.

"Mom!" Royce yelped.

"This 'training', is that combat training?" Jessa asked as she followed the other family members and piled food on her plate.

"That's correct," Jonah answered.

A silence came over the table as everyone enjoyed the meal. There were a few moments of 'mmm' and 'yummy'. Omni was desperate to get Jessa's attention and succeeded many times throughout the meal. After the meal, the family gathered around in the small living room by the cozy fire. Some had to sit on the floor. Jessa sat and observed how similar her family was to them, and it made her miss them more.

A few times, she discreetly wiped tears from her eyes and stared at the purple light upon her hand. She knew she wouldn't be able to put those tears in a vial, but it reminded her that she would have to meet up with Sami later. Grace got up to start some tea and Tristan followed her to the kitchen. Both of them started whispering. The rest of the family started a game, which Jessa found she really enjoyed. Grace and Tristan joined shortly after and handed out cups of tea.

Omni eventually showed strong signs of being tired, and Royce had already fallen asleep on the couch. Jonah got up and nudged Royce to get up and go to bed, and Grace took Omni to wash up. Tristan offered a hand to Jessa and recommended that they head back to his home for the night. They said their goodbyes to Grace and Jonah. Jessa felt her heart squeeze; she didn't want to leave. It was so peaceful and calm.

Tristan took the path out of the village, and Jessa followed behind him until she couldn't see him in front of her. She stopped. She had never seen it get dark so fast. She was used to sunsets and light disappearing slowly beyond the horizon. The sounds of the rainforest got louder. She looked around; everything was covered in blackness.

In the rainforest, it was as if someone had turned off the light switch and darkness fell. The moon was not able to get through the thick canopy above them, making it even darker. She held her hand in front of her face and couldn't see it. The darkness also brought sounds that made her skin crawl.

"Tristan!" she yelped. "Tristan! I can't see anything."

Without hearing a word, she felt the sure and strong pressure of his hand take hers. He continued to lead her through the rainforest as if he could see perfectly. He could have used the glow rock, but he chose not to. He knew the way so well he didn't have trouble navigating in the dark, though he preferred to navigate in the light.

"Where is the moon?" Jessa asked above the sounds of the rainforest.

"Moon?" Tristan responded.

"You don't have a moon? Doesn't it go hand in hand with the sun?" Jessa asked, not sure she was as good at astronomy as she was biology.

"If we have one, you can't see it from this Land."

"Why don't you use your glow rock to see, then?"

"The bugs."

"Bugs?" Jessa asked.

"They will attract to the light and then follow us right into my home."

"Oh." She fell silent.

After a while of trudging through the thick under-brush, they finally came to a stop. She would have collided into him if he hadn't stiffened his arm out to keep that very thing from happening. The rainforest was coming alive, and she wondered how they were going to sleep with the sounds. It started to get chilly and she shivered.

"I'm going to lower you down," Tristan broke the silence.

"Okay," she said quietly.

He turned her around so that her back was against his chest. Jessa held her breath; this was the closest she had been to him. She wanted him to hold her, to feel the comfort she missed. A war went on in her mind of wanting to keep distance and yet wanting to be this close to him all the time. It was amazing what she could feel after just one day. Although, according to the ship attendant, Anita, they had been on the ship for a few days as well.

Tristan whispered softly in her ear, "You ready?" He was so close she could feel the breath on her neck and his heartbeat from leaning against him.

She realized he was waiting for a response; she cleared her throat. "Yes."

She didn't know if she was imagining things or if she

was hoping that what she was feeling was as powerful for him as it was for her. His movements seemed to go in slow motion as his hands traveled up her sides and then across her arms. He stretched them out above her and lifted her. She felt her feet leave the ground, heard him hold his breath, and watched as the hole to his home came into view beneath her. She dangled over the opening; he didn't seem to be straining under the weight of holding her. Then he slowly lowered her down into his home.

Tristan dropped the chain with the glow rock down the hole for her to use. She put it around her and used it to look around the cozy area again. She rubbed her arms as the chill from the area settled on her. Jessa realized she was no longer tired, now that she remembered they would be sharing a room. Tristan landed right next to her.

"Are you okay?" he asked.

"I'm fine. I'm just not looking forward to another cold night," she answered.

"You don't have to be," Tristan reasoned.

Chapter 13

Jessa had no way of really knowing how much time had passed, but she guessed it was close to fifteen days since her family got on the ship. It felt much longer, and her days of missing her family were over-whelming and sometimes paralyzing. She and Tristan were still spending most of their time together; it was split between arguing and peace. There were times when she wished she could have the guts to find her own place to stay, but she still felt dependent on him.

Jessa had been working on some of the recipes that she found in the book Grace had gotten her. Some of the recipes she did in Grace's kitchen and other times she practiced some at the waterfall.

"I want to learn how you made that pouch that you gave me. Will you teach me?" Jessa asked Tristan one day while they were in the village.

"I will show you how to make one someday, but there is someone who is looking for you." A measure of worry came over Tristan's voice when he spoke the last part.

"Someone is looking for me? Who!?" Jessa jumped up.

"I believe it is your sister, Teagan?' Tristan answered.

"Holy crap! Hurry, take me to her," Jessa said as she gathered up her sarong, seashell, book, and vial. She quickly placed those things in her new pouch, put her sarong on, and wrapped her rope around her.

"She is over at the boulders. You have unique family members if they are anything like the two of you," Tristan said.

"I will give you a chance to explain that on the way there," Jessa responded shortly.

Tristan took her hand and said, "Would you rather get there faster or do you want the explanation—the latter would most likely slow us down."

"Good point. Take me to her as fast as you can,"

Jessa answered.

At that he didn't hesitate, and he pulled her along on a quick run through the rain forest, dodging low plants and big leaves. Of course, Jessa was not quite accustomed to dodging and got a few slices across the face from the leaves that slapped back from Tristan's movements. She was thankful for the leather beneath her feet, which seemed to protect her from most of the rainforest floor.

They cleared the tree line that went right up to the sandy beach. Jessa tripped a couple of times on her way through the sand, but Tristan's strong arm pulled her right back up. She was grateful for his strength and speed.

Niko and Naoki were already waiting as close to the shore as they could get. Tristan didn't hesitate and grabbed her hand again and pulled her through the water. She was surprised how he didn't slow even a fraction at pulling her weight through the water. Living near the ocean was an obvious advantage to building strong muscles for fighting the waves and other necessary things for survival. Jessa continued to marvel at his strength, even though she was moments from seeing her sister.

Everything went much quicker when Jessa was with Naoki. She quickly arrived at the boulders where several people were playing and splashing around. Jessa was treading water, her hand on Naoki, as she looked fervently around the area for her sister. She wasn't able to spot her right away so she began to yell out Teagan's name. It felt much longer than a couple weeks since she had last seen her. She thought back to the times she was away for college and didn't come close to missing her sister this much.

"Teagan!" Jessa called out.

"She won't be able to hear you over the noise," Tristan said, trying to calm Jessa.

Tristan swam over to Jessa and wiped at her face.

"First, what happened to your face? Second, are you upset?" Tristan asked softly.

"I cut my face trying to keep up with you in the rainforest. I'm crying because I miss her. I can't believe it, but it feels like it has been years since I have seen her," Jessa hiccupped.

"Well, she is here. No more tears, okay?" Tristan said.

"You're right," Jessa nodded.

"Let's swim over to the boulder, just relax, and watch for her," Tristan said as he helped her over to the nearest boulder.

They climbed the boulder and sat down for a moment; Jessa took a deep breath and shaded her eyes with her hand as she looked around. Jessa's heart was pounding at the thought of being reunited with Teagan. Her breathing was erratic. Her hands were shaking. She was so worried about her sister, wanting her to be safe.

"Distract me. This is too hard," Jessa panted.

Tristan pulled her close. "Do you see her yet?"

"No, and that's not helping." She paused and continued, "Why is my family unique?"

"Well, because you can heal and your sister can travel to any Land she wants without needing the ship or a piece from that land. I have no idea about the rest of your family, but I imagine they have some abilities we haven't seen in these Lands before. I am really curious how your sister got here, unless she did use the ship, but I haven't seen the ship since you came," Tristan explained.

"So, she might have some cool abilities too? That's awesome," Jessa said in excitement.

"Is that her over there?" Tristan said and pointed to the other side of the set of boulders.

"Yes, it is!" Jessa said and instantly dove into the water after her. Tristan was close behind.

The waves splashed over her as she did the front crawl over to where they last saw Teagan. Jessa swam up behind Teagan and gave her a big hug. Teagan squealed as she turned around to face her sister. Jessa had a big smile on her face and swallowed so much saltwater because of it. Teagan was splashing around her, animated in her excitement of seeing her sister. Tristan watched as the two girls screamed and talked really fast about the things they have seen and experienced.

He couldn't believe that people could talk that fast and still understand each other. At times they didn't even finish their sentences and they appeared to know exactly what the other was saying. He was flabbergasted. He tilted his head in wonder and continued to try to track their conversation, but he gave up after several squeals of excitement and a jumble of words he couldn't make out.

"Tristan, this is my sister Teagan." Jessa finally took a break and introduced the two of them. Teagan smiled in appreciation; Jessa knew that look.

"Nice to meet you," Tristan nodded as he continued to tread water.

"How long are you here for?" Jessa asked.

"I'm not sure. Do you know how long you are going to be here?" Teagan responded.

"Good point. Time is a little different and I'm not sure where I would go," Jessa said, realizing the conversation was getting serious.

"Or if we want to go," Teagan finished.

A wave washed over Jessa's head, she sputtered a little and said, "You want to stay in the Lands?"

"I don't know. I'm still trying to figure out what the Lands are. To be honest, I wanted to get the heck out of here, but now that I have you…" Teagan trailed.

"I'm not sure how you two are still floating with how much air you use talking," Tristan was barely able to interject.

"Grace told me that if we leave the Lands, we can't ever come back," Jessa said as she swam over to a boulder to hold on.

"Who's Grace?" Teagan asked.

"She's my mother," Tristan answered, happy that he could keep up with the conversation.

"You have family here!" Teagan said in bewilderment.

"Yes, I was born here. My whole family is here," Tristan said.

"Wow. That's cool. I never thought I would care whether my family was all in one place," Teagan said quietly; Jessa was barely able to hear her over the splashing waves.

The waves were getting bigger and more difficult for the three of them to tread water. It didn't help that they were pushing the group up against the boulder. Jessa was getting tired and could only assume that Teagan was too. Tristan didn't look the least bit fazed.

"We really should head to the beach. You have no idea how much I have missed you!" Jessa said.

"Good idea. I missed you too. But wait, who is that?" Teagan asked as she pointed at a man standing on a boulder getting ready to do a cannon ball in the water.

Tristan cut in. "That is Zeke. Why?"

"Because he is mine," Teagan said without hesitation.

Jessa looked at Tristan. "Is he mated?" Tristan just nodded as his face drained of color.

"Mated? What the heck does that mean?" Teagan asked.

"His mate is Julie; he has been mated to her for a while," Tristan said.

They climbed a boulder and sat up there for a while, breathing heavily. Jessa's heart was pounding in her ears. She couldn't believe her sister was sitting right next to her. A peace flooded her and she felt, for the first time in a while, things were going to be okay. Jessa put an arm around her sister and squeezed.

"You okay? Did you get hurt or anything?" Jessa asked her.

"It's been rough, but I'm fine," Teagan shrugged. Jessa's arm naturally came down.

"So, what does mated mean?" Teagan asked again.

"I guess I don't know exactly what it means to be mated... Tristan, can you explain it?" Jessa turned to Tristan.

"It means you will be protected and cared for," Tristan did his best to sum it up quickly, not wanting to go to deep into the details.

"Are they in love?" Jessa asked, changing the direction of the conversation.

"Wait, mated is different than love?" Teagan asked.

"Yes," Jessa answered.

"How would I know if they're in love?" Tristan chuckled and continued, "What would it matter anyway?"

Jessa didn't answer his question; she didn't want to feel the disappointment from his cavalier response to love. They sat there and watched Zeke jump into the water, a big smile on his face, and then he swam over towards Julie. Teagan looked like she was going to rip Julie to shreds with her eyes. There was obvious jealousy lurking there. Teagan turned away when she saw Zeke wrap his arms around Julie and they laughed together.

"Jealous much, Teagan?" Jessa joked and nudged her with her elbow.

"We ready to go now?" Tristan said, getting uncomfortable with the female craziness.

"Actually, can we go to the village? I am hungry and I wanted to talk with someone there. I want to introduce you to Tristan's family," Jessa said.

"Boy, have you gotten comfortable here," Teagan said with a hint of annoyance.

"Not by choice; she's wanted to leave since she got here," Tristan said gruffly.

"It appears everyone is settled in their Land. Micah is at Tech Land—loving it. Mom and Dad are with the Thornbergs, settling in Valley Land; it is very pretty there. I think it is really what Mom and Dad had pictured for themselves their whole life," Teagan said.

"You know where they all are? Are they okay?" Jessa exclaimed.

"They are all fine; Mom and Dad were concerned until I told them I was checking in on everyone. The Thornbergs have helped with their transition much more then what we have had. They are lucky to have more answers than us. Micah is having a blast."

"But what about you, Teagan? ...What pulled you?" Jessa asked.

"Nothing and yet everything. I didn't feel the pull anywhere the way it appeared everyone else on the ship had. The captain noticed and told me something about belonging to Oracle Land. I have no idea what that—"""

Jessa interrupted, "No! You cannot go to Oracle Land."

"I thought I would see your Land first, don't worry. So far I like it here... I especially like Zeke," Teagan said, surprising herself at how outspoken she was about him, a person she hadn't even met yet. Teagan decided she did not want to talk about how lonely and scary the trip was, seeing her family leave one after another.

"Let's get out of here," Tristan commanded.

He jumped into the water and swam toward Niko. Teagan grabbed Jessa's arm before she jumped in the water after him.

"Are you mated to him?" Teagan asked.

"Yes. At first I had the same feeling you do about Zeke...then I realized being mated does not mean being in love. It's frustrating to know that," Jessa answered.

"Hey, I brought our luggage with this time." Teagan laughed and pointed over at a boulder that had two luggage bags sitting on it.

"That is hilarious! Let me get Naoki and see if she can carry them for us without getting them too wet." Jessa laughed.

"Too late. When I jumped in the water, the luggage came with." Teagan shrugged.

"Alright then, but I still think Naoki can help carry it. We will drown trying to lug that stuff," Jessa said.

"What is Naoki?" Teagan asked.

"Let me introduce you. Stay here, I will get her," Jessa said.

In a few moments, Teagan was greeted by a beautiful, large killer whale. Teagan could not believe how large the animal was, and she was somewhat startled by how close it was. She screamed at first when she saw the killer whale approach. It sprayed her as a form of hello.

"Naoki is safe?" Teagan asked.

"Nope, I am just waiting in the wings here until she is hungry. It's a weird thing here in this Land...we wait to get eaten." Jessa laughed and continued, "Just kidding, obviously. This is my protector. We have a connection," Jessa said.

Teagan slid into the water next to Naoki and was surprised to see that Naoki wanted a rub on the snout. She chuckled and they swam to the luggage. Tristan came up behind them.

"What are you doing?" Tristan asked.

"Teagan brought our luggage. We were going to bring it to the island," Jessa said as she climbed the boulder. The luggage was really heavy with the added weight of water.

"I was hoping that Naoki could help with carrying it to the beach," Jessa said.

"She can help until it gets too shallow, but then what?" Tristan asked.

"I guess I will figure it out when I get there," Jessa said.

A few minutes later, Naoki was carrying the luggage as Jessa swam alongside her. Teagan was on Niko as Tristan swam beside him. Tristan wanted to keep Teagan out of the water as much as possible, in case a killer whale connected with her. He had no idea if that was even possible with how she got to the Land. He shook his head in frustration at how back-and-forth the Robinson females appeared to be. It took him forever to get them away from the boulders.

Teagan was laughing and having a blast on the ride to the beach, her wet, brunette hair flapping in the wind ever so slightly. Tristan noticed a resemblance between the sisters, and it did not get past him how beautiful Teagan was as well; however there were several distinguishing factors between the two girls.

He noted that Teagan had a green hue to her eyes and Jessa had a honey tone to hers. Their faces had similar shape, but their noses were slightly different. Their voices were similar. Teagan had a spunky personality—he caught onto that right away. Jessa seemed to follow the beat of her own drum and was very independent.

It was a struggle to get the luggage the rest of the way to the beach, but the three of them took their turns and by the time they reached a point where they could stand, they slowly walked up. Jessa collapsed on the sand and water rushed over her, but she was too tired to care. She launched her luggage up on the dry part of the beach as far as her noodle arms would throw—which truly wasn't far. Teagan followed her example and then lay back, taking deep breaths. Tristan walked over to Jessa to make sure she was okay and then sat down.

"I hope that was worth it," Tristan said.

"No idea if it was. I don't remember all that I packed. I know there are clothes in there. I'm not sure what condition everything is in, though," Jessa managed to say in between breaths.

"This place is so cool!" Teagan said as she got up on her elbows and stared at the ocean.

"Well it has its dangers, so be careful," Jessa said protectively.

Tristan did a double take as he heard the words come out of Jessa's mouth. That was a side of Jessa he had not seen.

"Yeah, I know. I have seen several Lands so far. This one is probably tied for first with how many dangers are here. But that makes it exciting!" Teagan said excitedly.

"You are one strange egg, sis." Jessa laughed.

"I can see why you left me for this." Teagan got serious.

"I did not leave you...I am so sorry, I couldn't stop the pull. Then I saw Tristan and I was jumping over the edge of the ship," Jessa said.

Teagan didn't know how to respond. She was frustrated that she was left alone, but hearing Jessa's side of the story made her feel differently. She wanted to blame Jessa for not being stronger and ignoring the pull. One thing she had learned while being on the ship is that no one could ignore the pull no matter how hard one tried.

Tristan just stared in wonder over their conversation, but as he listened, he couldn't help but have this nagging feeling that something bad was going to happen. Those feelings were normally confirmed, and he was getting a bit uneasy. He stood up and walked back and forth, looking over to the boulders and seeing Niko as close to shore as possible doing the same pacing as him.

"Something isn't right," Tristan said.

The conversation between the two girls stopped and both looked over at him.

"What do you mean, Tristan?" Jessa asked in a very serious tone.

"I think something is going to happen to Julie," he said as he looked out at the water as if looking for something.

Teagan didn't seem bothered by the fact, but Jessa asked, "How do you figure?"

"Because it sounds like Teagan is mated to him, but no one can be mated to more than one person at a time. If she feels a pull to him, then something is most likely going to happen to Julie. That is the only explanation." Tristan sounded concerned.

"That's fine with me," Teagan said.

"Teagan! How can you say that? Someone will be

hurt—or worse—die," Jessa yelled.

Teagan didn't respond.

Jessa got up and walked towards her luggage. She couldn't look Teagan in the eyes. She opened her suitcase and a majority of it was held in suspension with the help of saltwater. She took it and dumped it upside down and watched as all her belongings, from a life she had a feeling she never would see again, spilled out on the ground. Clothes gathered in the sand, two curling irons, a blow dryer, a makeup case, brush, and other toiletries. Her purse was on top of the clothes and ended up underneath the pile. She sighed in frustration and sat down next to the pathetic pile of soggy materials. None of it would be useful here.

Teagan continued to lie out and enjoy the sun, as well as take in the Land surrounding her. She was enjoying herself and thought nothing of the earlier conversation. She was happy to finally be with family after watching all of them disappear, even if it was just one of the members. Teagan learned a lot from the captain, but still didn't learn enough. When she found out that she could jump to any land she wanted with the use of her rope, she jumped to check on Micah and then her parents and left Water Land for last.

The captain had mentioned that he would be traveling

through the Lands again, but she didn't want to wait until he started his next revolution. The captain would be staying at Oracle Land for a while—that was where he lived.

Teagan interrupted her own thoughts, stating, "This place is beautiful."

Both Tristan and Jessa ignored her. Jessa continued to leaf through the remains of her belongings. Tristan walked over and sat next to Jessa as she went through her things. Tristan wanted to keep his mind busy to distract him from the hard thought of something bad happening again so quickly.

"What are these things?" he asked, pointing at the heap of things that required electricity.

"Well, this pile is stuff that won't work here. Umm, a curling iron to make my hair look nice and the blow dryer, there, is to dry it quicker; that is a phone and phone charger. None of those things will work here, plus the water damaged them," Jessa said. There was a small amount of sadness in the way she spoke about those things, as if it were a memorial to a life that she no longer would have.

"This other pile has things that I can still use: makeup, brush, moisturizer, and since I have some more clothes, I will use my handbag to pack those things and dispose of my luggage bag and electronics. Is there a place where we put trash?" Jessa asked.

"We normally burn waste. If you like, we can make a fire to burn these things, but if you would like to keep them, we can put them in my home," Tristan said gently.

"No, I don't want to keep them. They remind me of a life that was driven by society's definition of beauty and the necessity for everything to be ready at our fingertips. It is almost a promotion of laziness and shallowness," Jessa said profoundly.

"Whoa! What happened to you in the last couple of weeks? You become a tree hugger?" Teagan laughed.

"What does this do that it promotes laziness?" Tristan picked up the cell phone.

"Ah, now it is your turn for the questions. The phone has to do with laziness and this growing need to have things readily available within a moment. I can't count how many times I wanted to throw my phone because it was taking forever to load a video. A video! Really? I cannot believe that my life was consumed by that kind of frustration, when there is something like this that exists," she yelled as she looked out at the vast expanse of beauty around her.

"Interesting," Tristan said.

"What the heck is going on over there?" Teagan interrupted.

Teagan came over to where Jessa and Tristan were sitting. "What happened? And why are your tears purple?!"

Jessa quickly wiped at her face, not even realizing that she had been crying.

"Okay. Explain please. Why are her tears purple?" Teagan turned to Tristan and asked.

Chapter 14

Jessa looked at Tristan and then looked at Teagan and was about to answer, when a loud, ripping scream came from the other side of the boulders.

"This is too soon! This isn't right!" Tristan yelled out as he ran towards the water.

"Wait for me Tristan; I am coming with this time!" Jessa yelled out and chased after him.

"With what weapon, Jessa? Your bamboo stick?!" Tristan countered as he waded into the water.

"Give me something then...I am not standing here on the beach while more people get hurt!" Jessa yelled and swam out after him.

"You don't even know how to kill a snake, let alone the creature. You will die. Stay here!" Tristan yelled and grabbed onto Niko.

"Naoki!" Jessa barely had to yell out before she was by her side.

"Jessa, what the heck is going on," Teagan said right next to her; Jessa hadn't noticed that Teagan was following.

"We can't explain right now; time is really important. I have to go help. Teagan, please stay here," Jessa pleaded, but it was no use when she saw the look in Teagan's eyes as she saw a shadow over the boulders.

"Wh-what is that?!" Teagan shuddered.

"That is the reason you need to stay here and I need to go. Please, please go back!" Jessa yelled, swam out, and grabbed onto Naoki. Naoki did not hesitate and brought her to where the chaos was taking place, learning that she would go that way anyway without help.

"Naoki, I need you to go back and make sure Teagan stays away. Go!" Jessa gave the order, and it appeared that Naoki struggled with following an order that went against her own protective instincts.

"Go, Naoki!" Jessa said as she started climbing the boulders.

She found some rocks on the way up that she planned to throw at the beast. Then she laughed at how ridiculous the idea was. She didn't even know what the creature truly looked like or how big it really was. She tripped over a stick on her way up the last boulder. She couldn't believe that it was a sharp bamboo stick she tripped over; she figured the odds were in her favor and continued forward without questioning the possibility.

She crawled over the tallest boulder, huffing and certainly out of breath. She hugged the rock as she peered over the edge. She could not believe her eyes as she took in the scene below. The size of the creature was horrifying. People were swimming and moving as fast as they could, but not making any progress. She understood immediately why; the creature was making a visible current and it kept people from moving away, no matter how fast they tried to swim.

The creature was slick, slimy, and black with large scales; it was much larger than a blue whale. At this moment it was right underneath her, taking up most of the space in the cove that the boulders naturally created; where she, Teagan, and Tristan were just moments before. The creature focused on something right in front of it; Jessa tried to see what it was, but was unable to. She already saw what looked like scarlet ribbons in the water; the creature had already killed at least one person.

The few people that were on the boulders were able to climb over the other side and swim off towards the island. Jessa was still trying to figure out how she was going to help. The creature moved enough for her to finally get a view of what had been distracting it: Tristan.

Her eyes rounded in horror, and without a second thought she jumped off the cliff onto the back of the creature. She almost slipped off because of how slimy it was. The air was knocked out of her for a moment. She scrambled to catch her breath and gain better footing. It did not take long for the creature to realize that something wasn't quite right, and it began to move back and forth to figure out what was on its back. The thrashing made it difficult for Jessa to stay on, but she took the sharp bamboo stick and shoved it down into the flesh of the creature.

The creature began thrashing even more. Jessa was holding onto the bamboo stick as her feet slipped out from underneath her. Slimy, black stuff began to cover her as it oozed out of the wound she'd created. She knew well enough that the bamboo stick was the equivalent of a toothpick on an elephant; it wouldn't do enough damage other than to make the creature angry. She tried to get a better grip on the stick and began to pull herself back up; more than once she slipped on the ooze. Finally she got back up, and with all her strength she pulled the bamboo stick out and moved further up to the creature's head, trying her hardest not to fall.

Tristan was close to the creature's face, with several other fighters ready to take out the creature when the best opportunity presented itself. When it began thrashing, Tristan had thought that one of the fighters had gone ahead before the command, but when he looked up over the top of the creature, his heart almost stopped in his chest. Jessa was on top of the creature and she pierced it with a bamboo stick. He tried to ring in his concentration; one misstep with this creature and he was food.

"We have to make this quick, men!" Tristan yelled.

Just as he finished, he saw Jessa right behind the head of the creature, right at its neck. Somehow she was able to gain enough balance. He saw her take the bamboo stick in both hands, bring it over her head, and with wildness she screamed out and brought the bamboo stick down on the sweet spot of the creature. At that moment, the creature stilled as if paralyzed.

"Now!" Tristan yelled out and all six of the fighters and their killer whales dove underwater. Underneath the water, each fighter worked quickly with their weapons and cut along the underbelly of the creature, forcing the contents that to spill out into the water. The contents would make food for the fishes for weeks, but the skin of the creature could poison them, so it was important for the fighters to get the remains of the creature onto the island. They had many possible uses for what remained.

The creature heaved forward as the attack took place underneath it and Jessa, unaware of what was going on, was thrown against the bamboo stick. It pierced the side of her stomach. She looked down and saw the gash; red started to seep from the puncture wound. The realization that she was losing too much blood and probably wouldn't make it came quickly to mind. Her hand came away wet with more blood as she tried to keep it from spilling out. Dizziness overcame her and she lost her footing. She stumbled back and fell into the water, adding to the ribbons of red that were already there.

Tristan came up for air at about the time he saw Jessa fall back into the water and red blood surrounded her. He tried hard to get to her, but Niko was tired and couldn't push as fast as Tristan needed him to. Tristan sighed in relief as he saw Naoki seconds away. Jessa was sinking, which he knew was not a good sign. He was torn between taking care of his mate and finishing what he was responsible for. Then he remembered Teagan was there and she would be able to help her, if it was even possible to help at this point. The thought made him shudder and he turned to go back after her. Niko would not budge. Tristan was about to jump off when a voice stopped him.

"Tristan! Let's go; we have to get this done or the poison will seep into the water!" a male voice commanded.

The hard part would be getting the creature out of the water soon enough so that it wouldn't kill the marine life with the venom that was oozing out of the wounds. He knew he had a duty to his land, but the duty to protect Jessa pulled at him as he helped the other fighters.

Jessa felt herself sinking under the water. She didn't know why her body would not follow the command of her brain to move. She was hoping that adrenaline would keep her from dying. She fought the idea that she wouldn't make it. The sound of water rushing around her was so hollow and lonely. And then she felt, more than saw, Naoki around her.

Naoki brought Jessa as close to the island as possible. Teagan swam out at the first sight of Naoki and began to freak out when she saw that Naoki had a dying Jessa on her back. Teagan began screaming and pulled at Jessa. She got her off of Naoki's back and kicked like she had never kicked before, pulling Jessa as quickly to the beach as possible. Teagan began to freak out even more when she saw a stream of red flowing from behind them as she moved forward. Jessa was quiet and still, as if she had accepted her fate. Teagan was crying and screaming as she finally got Jessa onto dry sand.

For just a moment, Jessa opened her glassy eyes and muttered something. Teagan instantly shut her mouth and knelt down to Jessa and silently pleaded that she would say something that could help. Jessa muttered again.

"Louder, Janessa Avery! I can't hear you!" Teagan yelled and slammed her fists on her own thighs.

"Vial...my pouch," was all Jessa could get out.

Teagan didn't know what that meant but looked around and found a pouch secured to her by her rope. She instantly opened it and dug in. She found a book, which was somehow still dry, a seashell, and then a small vial about the size of her ring finger. Teagan had to guess that this was what she was talking about.

"What do I do with it? Do you drink it or do I pour it on the wound?" Teagan asked, hoping she would answer.

"P-p-p—" Jessa tried to answer.

"I'm going to guess that means pour and not drink." Teagan acted fast and opened the vial and poured it over the flesh that was pierced.

She emptied the entire little vial on the area; she couldn't help but worry that was not enough to do anything for it. Her worry quickly evaporated when she saw how quickly the wound was mending itself, from the inside out. She heard a sigh come from Jessa. Teagan watched closely as the wound healed completely. She wouldn't blink until she had confirmation from Jessa that things were okay.

"Jessa?" Teagan whispered.

"Hmm."

"Are you going to die on me?" Teagan's voice quivered.

"No," she mumbled.

Teagan fell back in the sand, not concerned about the tears streaming down her face as relief washed over her. Sand was everywhere: in her hair, on her shorts, and on her tank top. The sun continued to beat down on the beach. Teagan was curious how the sun could still shine after everything. The creature, from where she was, had looked gigantic and menacing. She drew in a deep breath and continued to watch her sister, knowing there was nothing else that could be done.

Tristan could barely concentrate as the six fighters and the killer whales pushed themselves to the edge of their strength, moving the creature to the other side of the island. Several hours later, they were able to finally get the creature on the island. Many villagers came out to help and began working right away to preserve pieces and parts of the creature. They needed to dry out the skin of the creature quickly so it would not leech into the sea.

They had a set up all ready to go for the next creature they would kill. This had been the second creature they had killed in all the time the Land existed, that the villagers knew about. They heaved the remains all the way to the set up place. Tristan was drenched in sweat and contained by a sense of duty, but his thoughts were elsewhere. His heart was pounding at the question floating around in his mind: *Is Jessa dead?*

Tristan left the villagers to do what they did best—harvest the creature for their uses—and he ran through the rainforest towards the beach where he hoped Jessa was. His feet could not carry him fast enough. Frustration and worry clamored up his muscles.

After a while, Teagan had gotten up and paced around the beach. Jessa had not responded for hours and just laid there. If she wasn't breathing and didn't have a steady pulse, Teagan would have been frantic. She was angry and frustrated that she had experienced yet another moment of almost losing her sister. It was too soon to relieve those feelings and thoughts.

The crash of the waves was the only thing keeping Teagan from losing her mind. She wondered several times where Tristan was, thinking as a protector he had failed miserably. She tripped a few times during her pacing but had made quite a worn path in the sand. Jessa stirred after a moment. Teagan didn't wait to launch into a string of words and questions.

"So what the heck was in that vial?" Teagan snapped.

"Some sort of healing agent," Jessa coughed.

"Okay well, I think it is story time. What was that black thing?" Teagan asked.

"I'm tired," Jessa tried and failed to sit up.

"You almost died! You can't do that," Teagan yelled.

"I'm sorry," Jessa whispered as her eyes fluttered shut.

"Now I see that I am going to have to stay in Water Land to keep you out of trouble," Teagan said and walked to the water to wash off.

Jessa felt around for her pouch and the empty vial that Teagan had let drop in the sand. Jessa knew she could fill it really quickly with the tears she had been holding back in front of Teagan. She opened the vial up and put it to her eye and let the shock of the day come in waves as she silently cried. She was right; it didn't take long at all to fill the vial this time. Teagan looked as if she was finishing up in the water, so Jessa put the vial back in her pouch, along with the book that Teagan took out.

She wiped at her eyes and saw Teagan on her way back, and then Teagan froze. Jessa followed Teagan's gaze and saw Tristan barreling down the beach towards her in a very fast, very angry looking pace. Jessa sat up slowly, finally gaining enough strength for the small movement. His figure was getting larger and larger as he continued down the beach, the sand apparently not slowing him in the slightest. Jessa could feel fear seep into her and her heart rate picked up. He looked very angry...and dangerous. In a second, Jessa was hauled off of her feet as if she weighed nothing, and then she was carried to the water. Teagan stood paralyzed at how quickly he plucked her up and carted her off. She couldn't even utter a word of protest. He was scary looking, and Teagan had no interest in getting involved.

"What is wrong with you!?" Tristan yelled as he brought her deeper into the water.

"I told you, I am a fighter," Jessa sputtered as water lapped over her, her body going rigid and almost preparing for another fight.

"No, you are not! You almost died!" Tristan yelled and dunked her underwater.

Jessa came up, spitting water and thrashing around, "What in the world is wrong with you? Are you trying to drown me?"

"No, I am trying to clean you off," Tristan reasoned. He couldn't stand the look of her blood all over her; it scared him.

"You have a funny way of doing it. I can do it myself," Jessa yelled back.

Jessa tried to get the blood out of her swimsuit, but

was unable to do so, but she was able to get the rest of herself washed off. Tristan just stood there as the waves swayed him back and forth. She had never seen such a menacing look from him before—especially directed at her.

"Go ahead say your piece; it's obvious I'm in trouble," Jessa said.

"How are you still alive?" Tristan asked in a tight voice.

"Have you forgotten about my tears?" Jessa asked.

"No, but you were practically dead before Naoki even reached you. How would you have been able to cry on your stomach!?" Tristan yelled at her.

"I'm sorry; are you disappointed that I am still alive?" Jessa asked. "I know you would prefer a woman that is less difficult to be mated with."

"That's not even close to it at all." Tristan's eyes softened only a little.

"Then please explain why you are so angry that I am alive and okay?" Jessa responded.

"You went against my command and you got hurt because of it. And you scared me..." Tristan said and continued, "You have someone to thank and apologize to." He nodded in the direction of the deeper parts of the water and then turned around and left her there.

"Naoki," Jessa whispered to herself. She swam out to where Naoki was swimming back and forth with obvious anxiety.

"Naoki, my hero! Thank you so much for saving my life; I am so sorry I put you through all of that. I have some work to do before I ever do that again," Jessa said to the killer whale. Jessa placed a kiss on Naoki's snout and told her to go to Niko.

Chapter 15

Jessa swam back to shore and saw that Teagan was crying in Tristan's arms. Jessa walked over to where her luggage and handbag were and grabbed them and then walked over to Tristan and Teagan. Her pouch was on the ground by them.

"What's wrong?" Jessa asked quietly.

Tristan answered, "She almost lost her big sister."

Jessa walked over to her and gathered Teagan in her arms, politely shoving Tristan out of the way. She rocked back and forth until Teagan began to quiet. After a few minutes, Teagan pulled away and looked at her sister. Jessa noticed that Teagan's tears were gold. Jessa looked at Tristan with a questioning look, and it was like he could read her mind.

"Those are the tears of an Oracle; royalty...like yours," Tristan answered.

"Does that mean the captain will force her to live in Oracle Land or Beneath Land?" Jessa asked.

"He obviously already knows that she is special, since she can travel the Lands without any need for the ship or a token. He hasn't taken her there yet. It may be because she is to replace the Oracle that is there; the current Oracle has an expiration date that is fast approaching," Tristan said.

"Now it's story time, finally," Teagan said as she sat down and wiped at her eyes.

"You also can see the length of other's lives...it appears. Julie was the only one that died today," Tristan said solemnly.

"Julie died?" Jessa asked in horror.

"Wow; didn't see that coming. If I am supposed to be some sort of Oracle, how come I didn't know that?" Teagan asked.

"I don't know," Tristan shrugged.

"He's in pain?" Teagan looked like her world was falling apart.

"Of course; they were together for a long time," Tristan reasoned.

"But it's not like they were in love, right?" Teagan said.

"That doesn't mean that he didn't care for her," Tristan responded.

"I can't stand the fact that he is in pain. Where is he? I want to be there for him." Teagan stood up and brushed the sand off of her.

"He is in mourning; he needs to be alone. He needs time," Tristan said.

"Where is he?!" Teagan shouted.

"I will not answer that. Teagan, he does not want to be found, and he won't feel any pull to you right now, since he is in pain," Tristan said.

"I think we should go and eat something; I am feeling a little weak," Jessa said, trying to change the subject.

"Good idea," Tristan agreed.

Chapter 16

The three of them trudged through the rainforest to the village, each carrying some of the luggage they had. Teagan was taking in her surroundings, much like Jessa did during her first time at the village. It was a natural establishment—all made out of the things the Land provided. This time the village was filled with a rancid smell.

"What is that disgusting smell?" Jessa asked.

"The creature. It is being harvested," Tristan answered.

"It was killed?" Jessa asked in wonder.

"Yes; the village doctor has done a brief autopsy to find out what was the killing factor, to help our battles with future creatures," Tristan answered.

"That's a good idea," Jessa answered.

"Zeke is here. I can feel him," Teagan interrupted.

"I am sure he is. His home is close by," Tristan said.

Teagan wanted to go to him, but thought better of it. "This place is full of surprises. There are healing elixirs, black creatures, mates, purple and gold tears, and killer whales as pets," Teagan listed off the things she had experienced so far.

"The killer whales aren't pets, they are protectors," Jessa shot back.

"Healing elixirs?" Tristan asked.

"Yeah, the stuff that I—" Teagan was elbowed in the ribs and given a dark stare from Jessa, making the message clear that she did not want Tristan to know.

"Nevermind," Teagan recovered.

They were about to reach Grace's home when Jessa excused herself and said she wanted to visit Sami.

"Jessa in the flesh! I heard about your heroics this

afternoon." Sami smiled as she saw Jessa browsing through her little home full of glass.

"Heroics?" Jessa asked.

"Oh, yeah, the whole village is talking about the death blow you gave to the creature. The doc was very stoked to find out where the creature's weak spot was. Somewhere just behind the head, on the neck area, right?" Sami explained.

"How did you find out all this so soon?" Jessa asked.

"The doc and I are close." Sami blushed.

"Oh, I see. That's cute." Jessa smiled and then handed her the vial she'd been holding onto. "Here you go, just as promised. Do you happen to have a wound right now, so I can prove its ability?" Jessa asked.

"Of course I do. Not that I did it on purpose, but it seems that I burn myself every day, or cut myself on glass," Sami said.

Sami held out her hand, a big gash clearly visible in her palm. She put a few drops on the gash and both she and Jessa looked closely and saw the gash mend itself from the inside out in a matter of seconds. Sami was dumbfounded and unable to speak for a moment as she tried to figure out how it worked.

"Where did you find the stuff?" Sami asked in wonder.

"I can't tell you that, but I did my end of the deal. Do you have more vials?" Jessa asked.

Sami held out her hand for the full vial with a smile. "Of course I do." Sami went to the back of her home and came back with a tray of vials, held up like little test tubes in holders; one had a chain attached to it.

"For now I will take two, and you tell me if you need more. You supply me with a lifetime of vials, and I will supply you with a lifetime of the healing elixir. A few drops work perfectly for small injuries as you had, but for bigger ones it may need a bit more. I have to stress that it is not easy to come up with this elixir so please do not use it too quickly," Jessa said.

When she was done at Sami's, she left to go to Grace's home. Someone grabbed her around the waist and brought her back into the dark forest. The breath was knocked out of her, and her heart picked up immediately. She looked around and saw another angry look.

"What the heck do you think you are doing?" Tristan asked angrily.

"I don't know what you are talking about," Jessa said evasively.

"You are creating business transactions with Sami—over your tears!" Tristan almost shouted.

"I don't think of it as a business transaction, Tristan, and what were you doing spying on me?" Jessa responded.

"I was not spying, I wanted to know what my mate needed that I couldn't help with," Tristan answered.

"I am thinking ahead...and it has worked out well so far—otherwise I'd be dead right now!" Jessa shouted angrily.

"Lower your voice, woman; this is a private conversation between mates and no one else needs to hear it. What is Sami trading for your healing tears?" Tristan asked.

"Vials; I need something to hold my tears in when I am not there to help," Jessa explained.

"Why do you think you won't be here to help?" Tristan asked quietly.

"What if the captain forces me to leave and live on Oracle or Beneath Land? What about the people here? Now that there is a way to heal wounds, I cannot just walk away without trying to help," Jessa responded.

"What is with your constant need to help, Warrior Woman?" Tristan asked with a smile, tears twinkling in his eyes.

"I have to... I can't explain it," Jessa whispered.

"Did you hear what the doc said about the killing blow to the creature?" Tristan tried to change the subject.

"Sami told me; yes." Jessa looked away.

"So, you are a hero, Warrior Woman," Tristan said with pride.

"Tristan, I know that you don't like what I am, or even who I am. So please don't pretend to be okay with it—faking it doesn't make it better for either of us. Let's just go about our business as if nothing happened. I am hungry and I am sure you are too," Jessa said as she pushed him back and walked past towards his mother's home. He followed behind her.

Chapter 17

Teagan was deep in conversation with Grace by the time Jessa and Tristan entered the home. Jessa wasn't surprised that Teagan drifted into a quick friendship with Grace—Teagan was always the sociable one. It was a relief, but at times she found herself jealous at her sister's ability to make friends quickly.

"Can you believe how amazing this woman is?" Teagan smiled as she pointed at Grace.

There was food on the table ready to be eaten. Both Jessa and Tristan smiled and joined Teagan and Grace at the table and ate as if it was their first meal in days. Grace was excited to meet Jessa's sister and opened her home for her to stay in until she mated. Teagan was more than willing, because it meant that she was able to stay close to her future mate.

Grace had gone through some warnings about not touching the ocean unless she planned to stay in this Land. Teagan figured she would be staying long before Grace told her, but she decided to follow the rules and use the waterfall as a place to play in the water.

After the meal, Jessa helped clean up. Tristan excused himself and left to take care of some things. Teagan was shown to a small area for her to use as her own, and she fell quickly to sleep. After Jessa finished cleaning, she asked Grace to give her directions to the waterfall; she desperately wanted to feel clean again— the saltwater hadn't helped. Grace gave her directions to a more secluded waterfall and gave her some soap. Jessa brought her handbag with her, with the plan to dry out the clothes that she had packed. Her sweatshirt was going to take the longest.

When Jessa finally reached the small, more secluded, waterfall area, she sat her things down on a smooth rock and took out her clothes. The sun was peeking through a little before its final descent for the day. She hung all her clothes on the trees that stretched out along the edge of the shimmering water. Knowing that she was alone, she took off her sarong and swimsuit and jumped into the water with the container of soap. She swam out to the waterfall and used it as a shower as she cleaned off the salt, sand, and any leftover blood. She marveled at how her tears had kept the wound from leaving a scar. No one would believe that she had a near-death experience less than a few hours ago.

Jessa cleaned her swimsuit and sarong and laid them out to dry as well. She laid out on a smooth rock, completely nude, trying to air dry. She knew her hair was an impossible mess. She had taken out the leather strips that Tristan put in earlier and left them out to dry as well.

Jessa held the vials in her hands as she lay there, knowing it wouldn't be long for the tears to form. She felt so weak with how much she had been crying lately. Jessa realized an internal struggle forming of wanting to be a Warrior Woman, as Tristan called her, but a Warrior Woman does not cry. The shock of the day and all that took place crashed into that one moment. She lifted the vials to her eyes when she felt the first sting of tears.

"Round two," Jessa said to herself.

It got a little chilly when the sun disappeared behind the trees, but Jessa wanted to wait until her clothes were at least somewhat dry...she hadn't been in dry clothes since she came here. A breeze picked up and she hoped it would help the clothes dry, but she felt the chill sink deeper in her skin. She hummed to herself as she heard some birds chirping above her.

Grace had told Tristan where she was when he went back to the house to show Jessa the leather they would use to make her a blanket. When he came up to the clearing of the smaller lake, he noticed her hanging clothes on the trees to dry out. He watched her for a moment and realized quickly that she was taking off all of her clothes. His eyes got wide and he struggled to look away, wanting to give her privacy, as it seemed this was her private time. He had no idea he would be intruding on such a private moment for Jessa. He justified his actions by telling himself that she was his mate, and eventually they would see each other naked. He looked away until he heard a splash and then she was under the waterfall scrubbing herself.

When she came out of the water, he thought she would get dressed, but instead she laid out. He was confused by her behavior, but figured she had no idea he knew where she was. He felt like a peeping tom, so he came out from the trees when he saw her shiver.

"My mother told me you were here. I brought something for you," Tristan said trying to look away from her.

"Tristan! What are you doing here!?" Jessa yelped and moved quickly to cover herself.

Tristan held up two very large pieces of animal hide in answer.

"Don't come any closer," Jessa warned, clearly mortified at the situation.

Tristan thought he froze, not realizing he was still moving forward to her. He shook his head; his body had a mind of its own. He realized he wanted desperately to wrap the animal hide around her with him wrapped around her too. He wanted it so bad that it ached in his heart. *What's wrong with me?* he thought.

"Can you toss me my sarong?" Jessa asked.

Tristan set down the large, heavy pieces of soft hide and grabbed the sarong and tossed it to her in disappointment. He wanted to tell her she didn't have to cover up because he was her mate and no one else was there, but he thought better of it.

"I'm your mate," he whispered quietly, more to himself, but he found she heard when she replied.

"I may be your mate, but that doesn't mean we will be doing the action of mating, if you know what I mean." Her breath caught at the hungry look in his eyes, this time he refused to look away as she tried to discretely wrap herself up in the damp sarong.

"Okay," he answered softly.

"Now, what is it that you brought me that couldn't wait?" Jessa gestured to the two large pieces.

"I figured you weren't too happy about the idea of sharing a bed with me, but you were very cold the last few nights. So, I brought some soft hide for us to sew together to make an extra thick blanket for you," Tristan said as he took out a metal object, and grabbed a big rock and some long, thin strips of leather.

She stood there for a moment, her hair drying slowly around her face. At any moment it would get frizzy and out of control. She wanted to ask Tristan to do her hair again the way he did before, but two reasons kept her from asking: one, he was already being so thoughtful about the blanket and she didn't want to ask for more; two, she was afraid of what the feel of his fingers in her hair would do to her. She absent-mindedly ran her fingers through her hair instead.

"Want help?" Tristan said in a low, husky voice without even looking up.

How did he know? she thought to herself. She didn't say anything as she continued to stand in the exact spot. After a moment of silence, he looked up at her, tilted his head, and raised an eyebrow in question. She nodded timidly. He got up from his spot and came toward her. She instinctively moved back.

"I can't do your hair from here," Tristan smirked, a little annoyed that she still balked at the proximity of him.

Jessa took a deep breath. "I was just getting the leather strips," she lied.

He moved toward her again and she told herself to stay still. Her heartbeat thrummed in her ears as it increased. She felt her palms get sweaty. She wondered why she was reacting this way; he'd done this before and it hadn't affected her so much. He reached around her for the pieces of leather. She could smell his skin, a mixture between soap and salt; she loved the way he smelled and found herself leaning in to it.

His fingers moved expertly through her hair; he smoothed it out and then began to weave the pieces together. He pulled when necessary and smoothed where needed. Eventually, she ended up with a professional-looking braid running down the center of her back, with leather pieces strung through the entirety of it. His movements had lulled her into a peaceful trance, but when his fingers stopped she snapped back. Disappointment crept in when his body moved further away and he went back to his other project.

Jessa watched as he laid out the large piece of hide on the rock she was sitting on; he placed the metal spike on the edge of the blanket and took the rock he had and pounded down really hard on the spike. Jessa thought for sure the rock would break, but it didn't. He struck the spike a few more times. She couldn't help but marvel at the way his muscles bunched and rippled in response. Then Tristan showed her a hole he made in the hide.

"This may take a while; I hope you didn't have any plans for the evening," Tristan said with a smile.

"Actually, I had plans to go clubbing," Jessa said with a laugh and then scooted closer to him to see more of what he was doing.

That got a weird look from Tristan, clearly not understanding the joke; he had never been clubbing before in his life nor would he know what it was from stories. She could see a sheen of sweat beginning to form on his forehead. She fought the impulse to wipe it away. Instead, she watched the project and tried to stare less at him.

About an hour later, Tristan had finished one side of the blanket. He was dripping with sweat by that point. Jessa asked if she could try the next row. He handed her the spike and rock and she wailed on the spike with everything she had. It took six tries to his three for her to get the spike to puncture the hide. She was tired out by the third punch, but refused to give in.

Tristan had gotten up and filled his canteen with some clean water, and jumped in the water to cool off; they both took a quick water break. The rainforest was getting darker and darker. The urgency of completing the project was heavy upon them. Tristan didn't spend a lot of time in the water and eventually went back to work. He took over after she completed the row. He blasted through that row quicker than the first one and kept going onto the next side. Jessa thought it was a cool design for a blanket, but didn't understand the purpose of the holes—she figured it was a cultural thing until Tristan took another pelt and place it underneath the finished one and aligned the two pieces.

He lifted his hand to strike the spike when Jessa interrupted, "You have got to be kidding me."

"What?" he asked.

"We will never get this done in time; it is already too dark to see anything," Jessa said.

"I will teach you that you don't need your eyes to see everything. But for now we can use my necklace to make sure things line up well," Tristan answered and with a loud crack the spike punched through the hide. He lined up the next hole and continued to do so until the two hides matched up perfectly.

"Now for the fun part," Tristan said in the darkness, putting away his necklace.

"Oh, really?" Jessa asked as she shivered in her sarong.

"Come over here, Jessa," Tristan commanded.

"I don't even know where 'over here' is; I can't see anything," Jessa responded.

"Follow my voice," Tristan said as he continued to talk.

She followed his voice and walked barefoot over to where she stumbled over him. He chuckled and pulled her down in his lap, and then turned her around so they were both facing the water with the blanket spread out on the rock right in front of them. The water sparkled as the stars glittered a reflection on the surface. No moon, but at least there were stars and the clearing was large enough to enjoy them. She shivered again.

"Why didn't you tell me you were so cold?" Tristan asked as he rubbed his hands up and down her arms, trying to warm her up.

Jessa was very distracted by his touch, but refused to allow her thoughts to wander. "So what is this 'fun part' you speak of?"

He stopped running his hands up and down her arms and instead followed them down to her hands. She could feel the callouses on his hands; they reminded her of how much work those hands had seen. He placed something in her hand. She ran her fingers along it, paying attention to what it was. She knew right away but wanted to take in the entire experience, using all the senses but her sight.

"This is a leather strip that we are going to use to weave the two pieces of hide together. We start at one corner and tie it off at the end of the other corner. I want you to follow my hands this first time so you know how to do it," Tristan instructed.

Jessa felt for his hands as they went to the corner of the hide and pulled the leather strip through. He fastened a knot on the end and continued to weave in and out of the holes that he had punched. Jessa was warming up, mainly because of the body heat that the two of them were sharing as she sat in between his legs. Soon he tied off the leather strip at the other corner, pulling the blanket toward them so they wouldn't have to move around. It made lining up the holes more difficult, but he didn't want to move from this blissful spot.

Finally he relented and decided they needed to finish the blanket quicker. Tristan handed her a leather strip and he grabbed one for himself. They both got up and worked on opposite sides of the blanket. Tristan finished much quicker and began working on the other side before Jessa finished with hers. She felt triumph at being able to sew together two pieces of hide in the dark. The silence continued as Tristan finished up the last side.

"You're right; that was the fun part," Jessa said, breaking the long silence.

"I think you should try it out now," Tristan said. She heard some shuffling and a then the blanket moved out from under her hands. Soon she felt a cocoon of weight and warmth surrounding her as the soft hide enveloped her in a warm hug. She shivered against the warmth of it.

"What do you think? Will it keep you warm?" Tristan asked.

"I think it is amazing. It is so heavy; I have no doubt it will keep me warm. What about you? Aren't you cold?" Jessa asked.

"Don't worry about me," Tristan said and began picking up pieces left behind by their work and shoved them into his pouch.

"Tristan, come here. Join me. After all that work, you should get to enjoy the warmth of this blanket too," Jessa said.

Tristan hesitated only for a moment before walking over to her on the rock; he motioned for her to get up. She followed him to a more comfortable spot on the ground, which was more pliable than rock. She settled down on the ground and he stepped behind her. He removed the blanket for a moment, sat down behind her—with her in between his legs again, and then wrapped the blanket around them. She rested her head back on his chest as he held her close. It didn't take long for them to warm up. Jessa could feel the exhaustion of the day encumber her, and her eyes got heavy. She wasn't the only one that had trouble staying awake. Eventually, they curled up on the rock and fell asleep sharing the big hide blanket.

Chapter 18

Jessa awoke to the sun shining right in her eyes. She felt pain in her back and side from sleeping in the same spot all night, but she felt warm. She sighed. Soon the evening before replayed in her mind and she remembered that she had fallen asleep out in the middle of the woods. Someone's rhythmic breathing broke into her thoughts, and she turned over and saw Tristan curled up next to her. He looked so peaceful sleeping there, as if he were sleeping on a comfortable bed. A lock of his sandy blond hair had fallen into his eye, and Jessa couldn't fight the urge to move it out of the way. Right as she touched his face, he startled awake, grabbed her arm, and appraised her like a stray animal. His eyes narrowed as if to size up his prey. Then realization came over his face as well.

"Sorry. Good morning," he said sheepishly.

"Good morning," Jessa said.

"I think it is my turn to take a bath. Where did you put the soap?" Tristan asked.

"Didn't you just take one last night?" Jessa yawned.

"Yeah, but I like to start my day off with one," Tristan reasoned.

"Over by my handbag," Jessa said.

"Wanna join me?" Tristan asked.

"I can wait," Jessa said quickly.

"I will keep my clothes on and you can put your swimsuit on," Tristan offered.

"That's a good idea, actually," Jessa said.

Tristan left the blanket and to Jessa's disappointment most of the warmth went with him. Jessa waited until his back was turned before she sprinted for her swimsuit hanging on a tree, and dressed behind a bush. A loud splash sounded from the other side of the bush and she assumed it was Tristan. As she looked over, that was quickly confirmed. She ran out and jumped off the edge of the rock into the water just a few feet from Tristan; she was hoping to get him with a big splash. She succeeded as she saw Tristan wipe water from his eyes. He was laughing. She laughed back at him and then caught a mouthful of water as he splashed her back. The splashing and dunking game continued on before they actually cleaned themselves with soap.

As Tristan was shampooing his hair, he said, "So, since you were the one that essentially killed the creature, a home will be made for you using the skin of the creature. Don't worry, though, the skin will be treated and won't smell bad at all. Actually, it makes for a nice home."

"It would be made in the village?" Jessa asked.

"Of course; it is a place you should take pride in," Tristan said.

"What if I don't want to live in the village?" Jessa asked.

"You don't want to live in the village?" Tristan asked.

"Not really," Jessa said as she rinsed her hair out in the waterfall.

"Where do you want to live?" Tristan asked.

"What if I don't have a choice where I live?" Jessa

countered.

"You are talking about the captain taking you from here," Tristan said more than asked.

"If I could, I would live in the rainforest in a secluded area that no one knew about, unless I wanted them to know," Jessa said.

"You don't think you have a choice?" Tristan asked.

"I'm afraid that I won't," Jessa answered.

"Me too," Tristan answered honestly.

They continued to wash and play in the water a little longer before they climbed the rock edge where Jessa's clothes were hanging. Tristan tried to offer help, but the independent Jessa wouldn't take it. Tristan had her sit down on the rock after she was dressed, and he ran his fingers through her hair again. Jessa closed her eyes at the amazing feel of it. This time he did a different type of braid in her hair that started at the top of her head; he still weaved leather strips through her hair and then wrapped it around the crown of her head. There was some hair up and some down, and the braid looked like a headband.

"You don't think that I like you?" Tristan asked as he continued to weave her hair into a tight braid.

"Huh?" Jessa asked, clearly not in the same mindset as he was.

"Yesterday you said that I don't like what or who you are. Do you really believe that?" Tristan reminded her, knowing this was the only opportunity he would be able to force her to talk.

"Why would I believe any different, Tristan? Our moment of being cutely matched, mated, and happily together was gone before we even made it to the island when I first got here," Jessa said.

"I recall you stating that you didn't like me, but I don't recall saying the same to you," Tristan argued.

"Don't worry; I wasn't waiting for any verbal confirmation—I had plenty of other confirmations," Jessa countered.

"Jessa, this is a ridiculous—" He dragged a hand through his own hair. "Why do we do this dance?" Tristan turned her and forced her to look in his eyes. Jessa could barely make eye contact with him; his gaze was so fierce.

"Perhaps it is a personality clash," Jessa offered with a shrug.

"I don't think it is a personality clash. I think there is more here than we are both ready to face. What if we have feelings for each other? That is what you want, right?" Tristan said as he continued to hold her face, forcing her to hold eye contact.

"Do you really think that two people that have those feelings for each other would fight as much as we have?" Jessa questioned.

"What if we are just fighting because we are scared?" Tristan offered.

"What are you talking about, Tristan?" Jessa responded and jerked her face out of his hands.

She got up and walked toward the trees where her clothes were hanging and began packing up her things, wrapped herself in her sarong—tied off with her rope and pouch—and hefted the heavy hide over her shoulders and took off in the direction of the village.

Tristan was not surprised that she had figured her way around this area of the island, and he followed after her. Jessa went right toward Grace's house to check on how Teagan was doing, and then she stopped right in the middle of the path and dropped her things. She stood paralyzed as she watched a new home being built with the skin of the creature. There was a smell that permeated the village and clung to the air that made Jessa's stomach churn. Tristan bumped into her when she stopped abruptly.

"Wow, look at that; it is much bigger than the other one!" Tristan stared in amazement.

"It's disgusting!" Jessa whispered with a shiver.

"It's an honor to have such a thing be used as a home when it has killed so many. It is essentially saying that the creature cannot have the power to ruin a home but rather make one." Tristan chuckled as he walked past her to help with building it.

Jessa continued to watch a while longer at the quick progress that was being made in erecting the monstrosity. She saw someone paint some goop on the skin; she figured it was the 'treatment' they used and hoped it would make the smell go away soon. She finally had enough of watching and picked up her things and went to Grace's home. The hide made her arms tremble, but she continued forward.

Jessa dumped her things at the door and walked in to a glorious display of breakfast foods and the entire family sitting at the table, including Teagan. She felt like she was intruding on a family moment, even with

Teagan there. Jealousy crowded her for a moment, but she pushed it away and moved toward them.

"Come and join us!" Grace jumped up to get another seat.

The family wanted to hear the tale of how she had slain the giant creature and all the gory details over breakfast. Jessa tried to tell it as excitingly as possible, but ultimately it was gruesome and a difficult fight. It didn't feel heroic; if she hadn't had the help of Teagan and Naoki she would have died for reasons she had yet to figure out. The subject of the home came up when Grace asked when she would be moving in next door.

"I don't know. Is it wrong to give the home to some-one else? Someone that may need it more than I?" Jessa asked.

Grace started tearing up. "You want to give it away? After all that you have done to earn it?"

"I am sorry—I did not mean to offend anyone, I was just wondering. I am so sorry," Jessa reached out to Grace.

"No, no... You didn't offend me at all. I just think that is truly amazing that you would fight for some-thing and not desire the recognition the home will bring. You would be among the higher class here in the village," Grace explained.

"Higher class? Aren't we all the same here in this Land?" Jessa asked.

"Well, of course, but when someone kills a creature it is a mark of honor that is highly respected," Grace said.

"Well, I prefer not to get recognition for something that turned out to be a fluke anyway. I had no idea I killed the monster until Sami told me. Heck, the monster almost killed me!" Jessa chuckled and reached for her cup of tea. An awkward silence came over the family.

Soon each family member took part in cleaning up and then separated into their responsibilities for the day. Jonah was sitting in a chair, working on a weapon of some sort. Jessa was extremely interested in how he was fashioning it and sat across from him to watch.

"How do you make those?" Jessa asked.

"A few key ingredients are important to making one of these." Jonah held up a sharp object that looked like an elongated knife.

"Okay," Jessa urged.

"The first two are the most important. Time and patience," Jonah said and chuckled at the look on Jessa's face.

"Right, and about how much time does it take to make that piece there?" Jessa asked.

"This piece, I have been working on it during my free time, and it has been several months. But it's not quite perfect yet," Jonah said.

"Why not make one out of the metal that made that hide punch?" Jessa asked.

"This is different. This is a blade that will not break easily or bend when under pressure. And it will not rust. This is made out of a special rock, found only here in this Land," Jonah answered.

"Where do I find this rock?" Jessa leaned forward as if she was being told the best story in her life.

"Jessa, your drive to be a fighter goes against everything the people of this Land are used to. Please understand that I am glad that you are okay and were able to defeat the creature. But you did go after the danger without thinking about the consequences," Jonah said, weighing the look in her eye before he continued. "Tristan has mentioned your inability to take direction from him and to stay away from danger. I'm concerned that you may have a passion too big to handle, and that may become a major danger to you someday. You have only been here for a short while and do not truly know this Land, yet you seek ways to be a fighter. I will not tell you where to find this rock; that will go against my son's wishes for his mate to be safe," Jonah said in a stern tone.

Jessa sat back and crossed her arms over her chest and watched him work the weapon piece. She wanted to argue with him, but found he was right. She did not listen to Tristan's warnings and had paid greatly for it. But there was a stubborn streak in her that she noticed as she thought to herself, if he wouldn't tell her where to find it, she could study it enough to find it someday. She didn't say a word after Jonah had somewhat reprimanded her.

Teagan interrupted the silence. "Jessa, you have got to take a look at your new home!"

"It's your home...not mine," Jessa said and got up to leave.

"What do you mean it's mine?" Teagan whirled around before Jessa left the home.

"I mean...I don't want it—so if you do, it's yours," Jessa said and hefted the hide and grabbed the rest of her belongings and left.

Teagan turned to Jonah. "Can she do that?"

"Looks like she just did," Jonah answered.

"Awesome! When can I move in?" Teagan asked.

"I believe it is being treated, so it may be a few weeks. You are welcome to stay here until it is completed," Jonah said as he continued to work on the knife.

"Thanks." She sat down and watched him as he continued to work on his weapon.

She watched him work so intently on the tool, and she wondered to herself if anyone would ever pay that much attention to her. She knew what she was thinking really didn't have any relation to what he was doing, but she couldn't fight the desire to be treated with so much care—the kind of care and attention that Jonah was giving to the details in the knife.

Chapter 19

Jessa didn't know where she was going, but she couldn't stick around the village as they made a home out of something that she associated with death and destruction. She stopped by Sami's and grabbed a couple more vials from her. After that she went to the only place she knew how to get to; twenty minutes later, she was on the smooth rock by the waterfall.

After staying in this land for over two weeks, it finally dawned on her that she needed a place of her own. She didn't want to share a place with Tristan, especially since she didn't even know how to get there. Frustration at what Jonah told her—how she was going against Tristan's wishes—made her want to find a place of her own even more. She wanted to punish

Tristan for what his father said. She realized it was foolish, but she was hurting.

Jessa realized the real reason she was hurting was that she had been messing up so badly that Tristan had to talk to his father. She wanted to be able to do the things that they did, and she didn't want to admit to not being able to do something. She also found she was scared of what she was feeling for him. Last night, the flutters in her stomach were not from being hungry for food. She was hungry for attention from him. She decided from that point that she had to distance herself before she got attached. If the captain were to take her away from here, saying goodbye to Tristan would already be the hardest part.

She looked around and liked the fact that most of her needs could be met by living close to the waterfall. Setting her belongings down on a rock, she began to climb a slope that led up to where the waterfall spilled over, hoping to get a better view of the area. There were jagged rocks and slippery points where she was afraid it could get dangerous. She pushed forward, being mindful of having a good footing before moving further. There were small openings in the wall of rocks and greenery that surrounded the waterfall; most of them were small and Jessa guessed small critters loved them. She continued to climb and found a good ledge that she was able to walk up a little easier. Jessa was about to continue forward when she noticed that there was a split in the rock that created a very narrow pathway; both sides were accompanied by high walls of solid rock and moss.

There were some spots that were completely covered by vegetation, at times making it dark overhead because of the thick plant life. She continued to walk cautiously down the path. She felt around and took in her surroundings as much as she could. It smelled like a glorious mixture of the waterfall, flowers, and plant life. She loved it and felt surrounded by comfort and began to think in terms of making this place her home, if she could find an ending to the pathway.

Light broke through an opening in the pathway overhead, and she found she was at a dead end. She spun around and found a barely noticeable crevasse in the rock to her right. Upon first glance, it looked like it was flush with the rest of the rock, but when she moved closer she saw that she could continue for another five feet before a big opening revealed itself before her. She wished she had a glowing rock like Tristan's, because she wanted to see if this was a feasible option for her to live in.

"Well, Tristan isn't here," she whispered to herself. She took a big gulp and went into the opening and used every one of her senses that were available to her to compensate for the fact that she couldn't see very well. She slowly went into the cave; she had to squat a little bit but not too much to get around in the cave. She started with using her hands and followed along the sides of the cave from bottom to top. She was almost glad she couldn't see very well into the cave, because she was afraid she would not like what she saw, if there were big spiders or other animals in the cave.

It didn't take long for her to make her way through the entire expanse of the cave. She sat down in the middle of it, smiling at her find. She also decided that she needed to find the caves where the glowing stones were so she could light her new place.

"Nice digs," she said to herself with a smile, her voice echoing a little against the walls.

Then she got up and left the way she had come, finding a safer and easier way back down. Jessa got her belongings at the bottom of the ridge, hefted them back up to the cave, and settled her things in there. She laid out her blanket and unpacked her clothes from the handbag and found a good spot to put them. Navigating in the dark was difficult, but she remembered what Tristan had said the night before about learning how to see without the use of her eyes. She changed into some more comfortable clothing: a pair of shorts, a tank top, and some flip flops she found in her luggage—which she managed to fit in her large handbag.

She was on the smooth, large rock at the bottom of the waterfall when she saw Tristan coming for her, looking upset. She faced him, having some idea of what might be on his mind. His pace quickened even more until he was right in front of her. The look on his face was pure anger, but it melted quickly into concern and he wrapped her up in his arms and hugged her tightly.

"I have been looking for you for so long. You have no idea how worried I have been," Tristan said as he squeezed tighter.

"Tristan, I can't breathe," Jessa huffed.

He released his hold on her, put his hands on her shoulders and asked, "Where have you been this whole time?"

Jessa shrugged. "Exploring. I want to get to know the island better, but I figured I would start somewhere that I was familiar with and work my way out."

Tristan responded, "Want some company?"

"I would, but if you want to be my company you better take a bath—you smell like the creature," Jessa said as she shoved him into the water.

Tristan was taken by surprise. "Well I need some soap to clean with, Jessa!"

"How do I make some for you?" Jessa asked.

"If you look in that book my mother gave you, there should be a short recipe for how to make some." Tristan pointed at her pouch.

"Oh, cool," She responded and dug into her pouch and pulled out the book. She was leafing through it and finally found pictures of the plants that could be used.

"Are those plants around here somewhere?" Jessa asked as she examined the pictures more closely.

"Yes," Tristan said as he dunked underwater.

Jessa went in search of the plants and a flower that would add a sweet scent. It had taken her fifteen minutes to find all the plants, and she came back to the small lake area and noticed Tristan wasn't in there. She looked around before starting to yell his name.

A voice behind her said, "I should push you in the water. Payback."

Jessa whirled around. "You better not! I brought the plants. I think I could make a great concoction of soap...but I don't have a container."

"That's okay; I made some while you were gone, washed up, and did some exploring of my own," Tristan said as his eyes narrowed at her.

"Oh...well, I suppose I could make some for myself later then," Jessa said, disappointed, as she set the plants down on the smooth rock. "Why would you send me out to get some if you were just going to do it yourself?"

"I figured you wanted to learn," Tristan said.

"Yes, I do," Jessa said.

"I'm learning your ways, Warrior Woman," Tristan said with a smirk.

"Well, that's not fair; I'm not learning any of yours," Jessa flirted back.

Tristan stepped even closer to her and then he took her hand in his and they laced their fingers together. Jessa looked up at Tristan and he looked like he was upset about something, but he tugged her off the rock and took her into the rainforest. Any thoughts of him being upset vanished as she was pulled through thick foliage. She slapped away the fronds that threatened to hit her face. Moisture gathered as water from the plant life kissed her feet and clothes.

About twenty minutes into the walk, she couldn't help but wonder out loud: "Where are we going?"

"Just pay attention to your surroundings, Jessa. It is a survival skill that will come in handy if you insist on being on your own," Tristan answered and pulled tighter on her arm as he quickened his pace.

"Are you angry?" Jessa couldn't miss the tone of his voice.

"I was angry when I couldn't find you, then I realized that I was more relieved that you were okay." He pushed a low hanging branch out of the way and continued, "I don't like it when you go off on your own. A creature as big as the one you killed may not live on the island, but there are other dangers here. I'm not angry...I'm...sad." Tristan shook his head.

"Sad, about what?" Jessa asked.

Tristan decided to change the subject: "I decided to name that lake."

"Sad about what, Tristan?"

He shook his head in response and continued to trek through the rainforest. A breeze wound its way through the trees and cooled Jessa's skin for only a moment. She found her clothes were drenched with a mixture of sweat and water that had nestled on the leaves from the early morning dew. Jessa wondered what he could be sad about. She thought back to their last encounter and all explanations escaped her.

"Can you do that? Doesn't it already have a name?" Jessa asked, figuring he really wasn't going to answer her previous question.

"I found out that you gave your home to your sister. You should still be honored for your bravery—even if it was against my wishes. So we will name your favorite secluded waterfall Lake Avery. What do you think?" Tristan turned around to look at her.

Jessa could not keep the tears from forming in her eyes. He stopped abruptly.

"What is it? Did you step on something? Are you hurt?" Tristan panicked and did a look over her to see where she might be bleeding.

"I'm not hurt. I am happy...these are happy tears. You would name a lake after me?" Jessa inquired.

"Of course; no one else uses that one—at least not as much as the bigger one, or the ocean. I could probably count on one hand how many times I have used that lake—and most of them include you," Tristan answered.

"I have never had anything named after me," Jessa said quietly.

"Well, I think it is very fitting that that lake is named after you," Tristan said.

Tristan tugged at her arm again and they took a sharp right and walked for another twenty minutes before they came to a cliff that dropped off into the ocean. The water splashed up high, but would never reach them; it was way too far below them. She looked down and saw jagged rocks at the bottom of the drop. Definitely not the place to practice diving. She shivered as the wind pushed wisps of her hair around. Tristan began walking along the cliff to a lower part of the land, and Jessa followed. They continued to follow along the edge until they reached a rocky beach, and when she looked inland she saw several small caves. Tristan looked like he was heading toward one in particular; Jessa tried to quicken her pace to keep up with him, but it was difficult with the jagged rocks.

They came to the mouth of a huge cave. Tristan didn't have to reach for her hand this time—Jessa entwined her fingers in his before he even thought to take her hand. He brought her into the cave and after one sharp turn to the left, it became dark. Tristan seemed to know his way around even in the dark. Another turn, and the cave lit up with a blue light; it was almost blinding. Jessa had to shade her eyes and realized that Tristan brought her to the cave with the glowing rocks.

"It's breathtaking," Jessa whispered.

"I figured you would need some of these to light your new home," Tristan said quietly.

Jessa turned back toward Tristan. "When did you...how did you know?" Jessa asked.

"I followed your smell to where you had been while you were getting the ingredients for soap. It looked like you set up camp in a decent place. Lake Avery— very fitting, don't you see?" Tristan tried to smile.

"My smell?" She smelled her armpits and continued, "What do you mean my smell?"

"You don't smell bad, but you have a certain scent, and I have gotten used to it. It's nothing creepy, it is just a skill I've learned when tracking animals and such," Tristan said.

"I see," Jessa answered.

"The important thing to know about these rocks is that they will not glow anymore if they are in the sun. Otherwise they will last for a long time. So you will have to put them in your pouch right away when you decide how many you want," Tristan explained.

Tristan hung back as Jessa looked at all the glowing rocks and decided carefully which ones she wanted to take with her. Once she picked out a few, she tried to pull them off of the cave wall, but they wouldn't budge. Tristan came up behind her and pulled out his knife and plucked off the ones she chose. She ended up with five beautiful, smooth rocks and placed them gently in her pouch.

"Ready to go?" Tristan asked softly.

"Yes. Thank you for bringing me here," Jessa said. She couldn't help but feel a sadness coming from Tristan, but she was afraid to press him about it and more afraid of his response. She didn't want him to tell her she couldn't stay there, and she didn't know if he would try to move in with her either.

Chapter 20

Tristan brought her back to Lake Avery, and without a goodbye, he began to leave.

"Tristan, wait," Jessa called out.

He stood where he was, but did not turn around. Jessa walked over to him.

"Please, talk to me," Jessa asked quietly.

Tristan turned around to face her, and she saw green tears fill his eyes. "I did not know you disliked me so much to find a place to live without me. I realized, now, that maybe we are meant to only be friends." His tears never spilled, but they were there, and Jessa felt her heart constrict.

"Friends. That doesn't sound much different than being mated anyway. You yourself said it was rare for love to be involved between mates," Jessa said after clearing her throat a few times.

"You are right. Friends isn't much different than being mated. Except one thing," Tristan said.

"What one thing?" Jessa asked as she swallowed hard.

Tristan came over so he was right in front of her, looked intently at her face, and didn't say a word—it was written all over his face. He didn't have to say a thing. His hand came up to the side of her face and he bent his head and pressed his lips ever so gently against Jessa's. Her mind barely had time to wrap around what was going on before her senses were assaulted by the greatest need she had never felt before. It didn't take much for the kiss to deepen and her arms to wrap around his neck. Her mind was reprimanding her for being so careless, but her body didn't seem to want to listen. It was the sweetest experience she had ever had, and when it ended so abruptly, she was left with an emptiness she couldn't explain. Tristan walked away after saying a muttered goodnight.

Jessa wrapped her arms around herself and shivered

against the chill that was quickly forming as night descended on the day. She was about to go up to her little cave home, when a sound froze her in her tracks.

"I thought you didn't really like each other," Teagan said.

"We're mated and that's about as far as it is," Jessa lied.

"Yeah, of course I'm going to believe that bull crap. I kiss random people that mean nothing to me, too. In fact, there was a baker that I just decided to kiss on my way over," Teagan said with a chuckle.

"What are you doing all the way out here?" Jessa asked, desperate to change the subject.

"Grace gave me directions to this place if I wanted to wash up, and she said I could probably find you here. Turns out she was right on both; this is a great looking spot to clean up, and here you are," Teagan said as she started to undress.

"Isn't it a little cold out now to jump in?" Jessa asked.

"Probably, but I smell. I suppose it is too much to ask that there are soap dispensers over by the waterfall?" Teagan joked.

"I can make you some soap," Jessa said as she looked

at the wilting plants she had gathered before the trek to the glowing caves. She took out her book and tried to read the directions, realizing it was too dark. She grabbed one of the glowing stones and used it as a flashlight as she read through what she needed to do. She looked around for a place to make the concoction.

"I don't have a place that I can mix these things together," Jessa called out as Teagan was splashing around in the water.

Teagan swam over to the edge where a gathering of smooth rocks settled. "Hey, how about right here? There is a little rounded out spot, like an eddy. You could mix your stuff in there."

Jessa looked where Teagan was pointing and climbed down with her things to see what she was talking about. It was right on the ledge of a big boulder that lined the water—the water being six inches below the spot. She saw the rounded out spot and began working on the ingredients, using her hands to mix it together. After some effort, she finally had a goop formed. A little more effort and she had a cream worked together, and Teagan was able to use it to wash up.

"Wow; that smells good! What else have you learned to do since you got here?" Teagan asked as she lathered the soap in her hair and around her.

"Considering how short a time I've been here, I guess I have learned quite a bit. It doesn't feel like it, though," Jessa answered.

"So, do you think I should stay here? At this Land?" Teagan asked.

"I would love it, but ultimately it is your choice. If that one guy is your mate, though, think about what you will be taking him from—this is his home. He's already lost his mate," Jessa answered.

"I'm well aware of his previous mate. I don't like that he had someone before me," Teagan said angrily.

"Well, on the bright side, being mated doesn't mean the same as being in love. Tristan had someone before me, too," Jessa offered.

Teagan came back to the ledge for more soap and continued to wash up as Jessa counted off all the things she had learned in the time that she had been there. Jessa wondered for the first time what had happened to Tristan's previous mate. No one talked about it. She thought that was odd. Before she could think more about it, she heard Teagan's voice.

Teagan decided that she was ready to talk about her time on the ship. "It wasn't easy, you know...seeing all the family members jump off a ship without any explanation. There was no one left by the time the ship made its full stretch. The captain sat me down and explained quite a bit about what was going on, since everyone else seemed to have found a place. It seems like the story of this place unfolds as people end up in each Land."

Jessa had to wait until Teagan returned before she could ask, "What is the story? What is this place?"

"Oh, Jeeze, like the captain would ever share that information with me. My guess is that this is an alternate universe; or we are caught between two different times. I honestly couldn't tell you how long we were on that ship before we came to Forest Land. Needless to say, I'm glad I came back here. This place is amazing," Teagan said excitedly.

"Do you think you could fall in love with him?" Jessa asked with a smile. Jessa could not recall a time that Teagan got excited about a guy before.

"I hope so." Teagan smiled back.

Teagan got out of the water and tried her best to air dry; she was shivering and Jessa felt bad for her, but she'd been warned. Teagan sat down close to her in her undergarments and drip-dried the rest of the way. Jessa braided Teagan's hair and used a piece of vine to tie it off at the end.

"How do you get your hair so beautifully braided, especially with those leather strips weaved in?" Teagan asked her.

"Tristan does it," Jessa answered.

"He what?" Teagan sounded shocked.

"Yeah, I didn't know that he could do it until one day he just did it to pacify me, because I was worried about impressing his family. Although I think I ruined any chance of impressing them," Jessa said sadly.

"What do you mean you think you ruined your chance of impressing them? You are all that they talk about, and with deep pride," Teagan said.

Jessa gave Teagan a smile. She was trying to be reassuring, but Jessa didn't believe her. Her conversation with Jonah led her to believe otherwise.

"Well, I better head back before I can't find my way. You coming?" Teagan asked.

"No, I know my way back. I have a place to stay for the night."

"Oh, yeah, I suppose—with Tristan." Teagan smiled, and Jessa didn't feel like correcting her. They hugged and said goodnight.

Jessa stood for a moment, looking at the water glitter in the moonlight. She couldn't believe that in just a few weeks her life had taken such a drastic turn. Never had she imagined there would be a place that was as beyond an explanation as The Lands. Jessa hadn't been one to dismiss the possibility of aliens or life on other planets; she even enjoyed watching the shows about them. That had been the closest explanation she had come to since the ship left the depot in its unexplainable glory.

She sighed and continued to have a rebellious urge to reject the fact that she was somewhere she couldn't figure out. She shook her head at herself and finally gathered her things and made the trek up to her new cave. This time she was able to see inside it with the glowing stones. She took them out once she got to a point where she couldn't see and navigated her way to the opening of the cave. The ceiling of the cave at the opening forced her to bend over a little, saving herself a headache and a bump on the head.

The cave had some areas that Jessa was able to create into shelves. She dug at them and used other rocks in the cave to scrape the surface to make them more smooth. She placed the glowing rocks in different parts of the cave to illuminate any shadows. It felt cozy. She looked around with satisfaction before turning to get her clothes for bedtime.

She changed out of her clothing into a pair of pajamas she had packed for the trip several weeks ago. She recalled with little difficulty the conversation where her mother told her to pack for all kinds of weather. She picked up the stones from the corners of the cave, put them in the pouch, and curled up in her heavy blanket. She left one stone out as a nightlight in case she got up in the middle of the night. Her eyes drifted low and she fell fast asleep.

Jessa had been sleeping for several hours when the snap of a twig sprung her awake. She bolted upright; sweat began to form on her forehead. She tried to be very still, and it didn't take long for her to realize she was holding her breath and her heart was pumping very fast. She listened longer and heard some rustling of plant life above her and a low growl at a short distance.

Jessa gripped her blanket tightly to her, paralyzed by a fear she had never experienced before. The sound continued for a while, but she reasoned that it was above her and not that close to the cave. Then she chuckled to herself as she remembered the first night when Tristan played tricks on her to frighten her. She instantly relaxed, took a deep breath, and snuggled back into her blanket and fell back asleep.

"Jessa!" Tristan yelled. He could not explain the horror he felt come over him when he saw a giant bear right outside of the cave opening early that morning. With the fear and the adrenaline coursing through him, he found the closest thing to him that could be used as a weapon. By screaming Jessa's name, he knew he had gotten the attention of the bear. He was hoping it would be the thing that saved her. Tristan couldn't spend much time thinking about that;the bear was looking directly at him.

He lunged forward with a scream and held his weapon up. He didn't waste any time; he plunged the sharp object into the bear. The first time it did not go deep enough. The bear managed to claw Tristan in the shoulder. The pain shot through him, but he did not stop. Any amount of time was too precious at this moment.

The bear growled and continued to thrash out at Tristan, only catching him a couple of times. The wounds were enough to start slowing him down. He grabbed the knife he'd worked on for several days from his pouch, and without much more time he had to make a move. He crouched low, surprising the bear as it had anticipated him standing upright. Tristan went quickly and shoved the knife in the low side of the bear's belly and gripped hard. The bear yelped out in pain and Tristan moved the knife vertically until he saw blood cascading down his arm and knife. The bear toppled over and growled in pain, but after a few short moments it made no more noise. Tristan made sure to give the bear a killing blow to keep from a long death.

Tristan climbed over the carcass and into the cave, still yelling, "Jessa!" He tried to give himself time to adjust to the darkness in the cave. Blood was dripping off of his arms, but at the moment he did not care. He feared Jessa had been killed. There was a little movement towards the back of the cave. He grabbed his necklace with the glowing stone and was able to see a little mound underneath the blanket they had made. He approached the heap in caution, afraid of what he might see. He knew he wouldn't be prepared for any possible nightmares involving Jessa.

He gently shook the bundle a little and said her name again. All of the sudden a body bolted upright and he saw a very angry look.

"That is it, Tristan! No more games of trying to scare

me all night. I was actually doing quite well all by myself until you started making noises and then roaming around in this cave! You have to stop it; it isn't fair that I can't get a good night's rest for once!" Jessa yelled at him.

"Are you okay?" was all Tristan said.

"Are you listening to me, Tristan? Stop playing practical jokes on me! You had me really scared for a moment there when you pretended to be some sort of animal and nudged me," Jessa said.

"What are you talking about? I just got here a few moments ago. I wanted to see if you wanted to go check on Naoki to see if she is doing okay after that bit with the creature," Tristan said.

"What?!" Jessa said in alarm.

"Wait, you...you thought that I was playing a trick on you all night long? Jessa, when did those noises start?" Tristan asked.

"I don't know, in the middle of the night...I just fell back asleep and they started up again and...I thought it was you." Jessa really looked at Tristan for the first time and saw he was drenched in sweat and something red. She shuddered at the thought of what it might be. He looked disheveled and exhausted.

"Not a joke. It wasn't me. You had a very curious and dangerous visitor last night. It is very possible that this cave had an owner before you claimed it as your own," Tristan said.

"Wh-what was it?" Jessa asked, obviously not seeing the heap near the cave opening.

"A bear," Tristan said, his anger visibly rising at the situation.

"No way," Jessa responded, disbelieving.

"Well, there is a dead bear at the cave opening to prove that I can't make this up." Tristan pointed towards the opening.

"I could have died!" Jessa yelled.

"You just now realize that it isn't a good idea to be off on your own?" Tristan asked.

"No, I realize now, more than ever, that I need to learn more than just survival skills, but fighting skills too...and quickly," Jessa said as she got up from bed. Tristan blushed as he saw Jessa was only dressed in a pair of skimpy shorts and a tank top. It was more than her swimsuits, but for some reason it felt different.

"Well, what do we do about that massive heap of

tiger food?" Jessa tried to sound calm.

"I will take care of it. Perhaps you should go to the village and eat breakfast with my family and I will meet you there in a few hours," Tristan offered.

"Tristan, are you okay?" Jessa turned back and reached out to him.

He nodded; he didn't move forward.

"You have cuts everywhere!" she exclaimed.

Tristan shrugged. "I am going to go wash off soon."

"Let me heal them?" Jessa asked.

"After I am done moving the bear."

Just then, Jessa realized she was standing there in her pajamas, and then to top it off she remembered the kiss they shared last night. She felt herself blush immediately. She tried covering up the embarrassment by searching for an outfit to wear. She grabbed her swimsuit—since there was mention of going to the ocean—a tank top, and jean shorts. She was thankful for her flip flops, because they would save her feet from further, unnecessary pain. Tristan left for the entrance of the cave and began to do some sort of care with the bear that she was not familiar with. Obviously the thing was dead. She shuddered at the thought of a bear poking around in her new home, and how close she was to being in danger.

Chapter 21

At breakfast everyone seemed overly quiet. Jessa tried to concentrate on her food, and Teagan tried to get conversation rolling, but both were unsuccessful. Jessa looked around the table and noticed Grace, for the first time, was not smiling. It was unsettling. Jessa didn't hesitate to help clean up after everyone was finished.

"How is your new house coming along?" Jessa asked Teagan as they were doing the dishes.

"The house still smells, but they got the skin completely covered with that treatment stuff." Teagan chuckled and continued, "Now we just need to stop off at Ikea and pick out some contemporary pieces."

Jessa couldn't help but laugh out loud—she couldn't stop until tears were streaming down her face and she was almost rolling on the floor. She was thankful for the opportunity to laugh, as the house has been so depressing this morning. She gasped for breath just to laugh some more. Teagan was laughing along with her.

"What is so funny?" Tristan came into the house.

Jessa jumped up from the floor and both she and Teagan answered, "Nothing."

"Well, your bear is now getting prepped to be a great rug for your place," Tristan said as he grabbed some bread to snack on.

"Bear? What bear?" Teagan asked.

"I had a visitor last night," Jessa answered quickly.

"Now, we have some bear meat for the village. There are several villagers that are thankful," Tristan said.

"There was a bear at your place?! Why would a bear go near that hole in the ground now after so many years of never having a visitor?" Tristan's little brother asked. Jessa turned red and looked down.

"Royce, I need your help with some trading at the neighbors; ready to go?" Jonah interrupted.

"Huh? Ah...sure," Royce answered and started after the door, following Jonah.

"Sorry about that, Jessa," Grace said quietly.

"There isn't anything for you to apologize for," Jessa whispered.

"What is going on here?" Teagan asked.

"Nothing. Omni, come on; let's go pick some herbs for today's meal," Grace said and grabbed Omni's little hand.

Jessa turned to Tristan. "Is that why your family has been quiet this morning? You told them?"

"Told them what?" Teagan interrupted.

"They found out when they stopped by last night," Tristan answered.

"Where were you last night, Jessa?" Teagan asked.

"My place," Jessa answered.

"Your place? I thought you shared a place with Tristan. No wonder Jonah and Grace were quiet all morning!" Teagan said.

"Last I checked, Teagan, this was none of your business," Jessa responded.

"Last I checked, we weren't on Earth, which means you don't get to be 'miss independent' anymore! You hurt people by your actions and you don't even think about it," Teagan said as she slammed the door on her way out.

Jessa ran her hand through her hair. "This is ridiculous."

"I'm sorry." Tristan cleared his throat, feeling awkward at Teagan's outburst.

"What do I do now? I seem to be messing up a lot." Jessa's eyes welled up.

Tristan started toward her but stopped; he didn't know how he should handle her at the moment. The kiss the night before was beautiful and a promise of something great, but only if she allowed it. He didn't want to push her. Every time he tried to get close, she seemed to put up a wall. She hid behind her desperate need to be independent.

"Want to go to the ocean?" Tristan asked, in efforts to both change the subject and make her happy.

"Yes, please," Jessa said, wanting the conversation to be over.

Once the salty smell filled her lungs, Jessa took off running toward the water. She ran as hard as she could through the sand, and on the way she managed to get her tank top off and flip flops abandoned. The only thing that slowed her down was her shorts. By the time she hit the water, she was only in her swimsuit. She swam out as far as she could. The waves tossed her around a little, but she enjoyed the ocean too much to care. Tristan popped up right in front of her, making her scream from his sudden appearance.

"I'm sorry," Tristan apologized again.

"Sorry for what? Apparently I'm the one messing up things left and right," Jessa responded.

They were treading water for a while before Tristan said, "I think I need help."

"Help with what?" Jessa asked.

"I don't know how to be what you want."

Jessa sighed and, after a few waves passed under them, she answered, "Tristan—"

"All I want to do is learn how to make you happy, Jessa," Tristan interrupted.

"It's my fault; I don't want to depend on anyone, especially for my own happiness. I can't expect you to be the one to make me happy. I have learned, growing up, the only one I can truly depend on is myself. It's difficult to change that way of thinking," Jessa attempted to explain.

By this time, both Niko and Naoki had joined the two of them and they were sitting on the whales' backs. There was a silence between them. Jessa didn't know how to cure it and the feeling of disappointment that was permeating the air around them. She gripped Naoki, and lay flat on the whale's back, and Naoki dove under the water as Jessa held tightly and tried her best to clear her ears quickly. Naoki made sure not to go to a depth that would be dangerous for Jessa. Shortly after the underwater games, they had surfaced and Jessa was having fun with her own personal wave-runner in the form of a whale. She couldn't keep a smile from breaking across her face. She called out in whoops of laughter, at times throwing her arms in the air.

After a while, Naoki and Jessa took a break and floated slowly along. She saw Tristan coming up alongside her and then he jumped in the air and landed right next to her. He pulled her into the water, and they swam together as they watched Niko and Naoki show off.

"Wanna go to the boulders?" Tristan asked.

"Not yet. It seems that place holds mostly bad memories for me now," Jessa said.

"Then all the more reason to go there and make new memories. I still have good memories there. One of my favorite is seeing you for the first time," Tristan said.

"That was a good memory. I hate that the creature clouded that for me," Jessa said as she swayed with the waves.

They both swam the rest of the short way to the boulders and climbed one of the ledges. The sun was beating down and warming up the rocks. Jessa was enjoying the breeze along the water and the warmth of the sun when Tristan asked, "Where is your rope and pouch?"

Jessa looked up innocently. "Oops."

"You forgot it?" Tristan asked.

"Yeah. I'm sorry, I did," Jessa said.

"We should probably go back and get it," Tristan said

as he started to get up.

"Wait. Why do we have to go get it just to come back? We can spend some more time here and then go get it," Jessa reasoned.

"Okay, but I was thinking maybe you would like to go to another land today—to see what it is like," Tristan said.

"Are you sure that is a good idea right now?" Jessa asked and continued, "My sister just got here. Since she told me that the rest of the family is happily situated, I don't feel pressured to leave as much."

"It's your choice," Tristan shrugged.

"Maybe Teagan would like to come with us?" Jessa asked.

"I think she might be curious, like you," he said and then changed the subject: "So what is it like where you come from?"

Jessa looked over at Tristan and blinked a little as her mind went back to a place she hadn't thought of for a while. She remembered a time where she had classes, homework, goals, internships, and responsibility. She thought back to a place where her moments were measured by a clock and time was money, a society that said your best wasn't good enough because there was always someone that could do better.

"That is difficult to answer, because most of what we had there is not what you have here. There are buildings, cars, highways, mansions, and a lot more things that you have never seen. To describe it would be as if someone described this place to me...only at least I have seen pieces of this where I am from," Jessa said as she looked at Tristan.

"I understand. I wish there was a chance I could go there and come back. The captain won't let us leave and come back, though," Tristan stated.

"I know, although I wonder why?" Jessa said.

"Well, if you think about it, you wouldn't be able to talk about this place with anyone, otherwise they will think you are crazy," Tristan reasoned.

"I would get institutionalized. That's funny," Jessa chuckled.

A moment of silence passed between the two of them before Jessa got the courage to ask, "Why don't you want to talk about Cade?"

He appeared to be taken aback by the question, and he didn't look like he was going to answer. His eyes narrowed for a moment, and his brow furrowed. He looked as if he didn't want to go that direction. Another moment passed until he answered, "I don't know why you want to know about him."

"It didn't seem like a big deal to ask about him, but now that you are avoiding the subject, it makes me more curious," Jessa responded.

"Cade was my best friend. He killed my mate," Tristan said with no emotion.

"What?" Jessa was shocked.

"It was a while ago. When I was mated for the first time, Cade and I were hanging out all the time. Naturally, he met my mate at the same time I met her," Tristan said.

Jessa struggled with jealousy as he talked about meeting his previous mate for the first time. She realized it was similar to the first time she met him. There was a sinking feeling in her heart as she realized their first meeting wasn't as special as she had originally thought. He had been there, done that.

Tristan continued, "My mate, Tania, had an ability kind of like you and Teagan. Cade had told her about going to Beneath Land and living with royalty. She didn't respond the same way you did and instead was really excited about the idea. She wanted me to move with her there."

"You didn't want to," Jessa filled in the blanks.

"I'm not sure if I would have, the way I would do anything for you." Tristan shook his head. "One day I wake up and the doctor tells me my mate had been in an accident and died. I haven't seen Cade since then, either."

Jessa was able to see he was getting frustrated as he was telling the story. She had the urge to hold his hand, and instead of fighting it she gave in. Once her hand was in his, she felt a jolt. Tristan looked down at their hands, apparently feeling something similar, and she could visually see him relax. It was a heady sense of power she got from that moment—feeling as if she could help him calm down.

"So, do you think Cade is somewhere in one of the Lands?" Jessa asked.

"Yeah, I think he is hiding out somewhere. He is very resourceful," Tristan's eyes narrowed.

"What if you saw him again?" Jessa pressed.

"I have no idea what I would do if I saw him again, I would rather not find out," Tristan said.

"Have you figured out why he killed your mate?" Jessa asked.

"No. I have not gone searching for him or answers either. I guess, now that I have you, I might need to get some answers. I don't want him coming after you, too," Tristan responded.

Jessa pulled her hand away and looked down She felt ashamed of her behavior at the beginning, and even now. The fighting to be independent was causing an unnecessary strain even with the recent events—she didn't see the point anymore, now that she had seen how much her actions impacted Tristan.

"What's wrong?" Tristan asked, catching the change in her behavior.

"I'm so sorry. I haven't been very good at...well, any-thing. I'm just, I'm sorry," Jessa said, tears forming in her eyes.

"Jessa, don't cry. We're a team; you just have to think like that. Instead of thinking I'm trying to take away your independence—it doesn't make sense—but I want to be a part of your independence," Tristan said as he put a comforting arm around her, which only forced the tears to fall.

"You're right, that doesn't make sense," Jessa made light of the heavy conversation.

Tristan couldn't help but chuckle. "My desire to make you happy far outweighs my reluctance to play with fire. Cade is dangerous. I don't want him to kill my true mate, but I will go with you wherever you want to go, I can protect you."

Jessa's head snapped up and she looked at Tristan. He had a crooked smile on his face, where one corner pulled up farther than the other. She loved that smile; there hadn't been enough times that she had seen it. She felt herself warm from the inside out at his statement of her being his true mate. The moment was coming to a close much too soon.

"I probably should see if Teagan is still mad at me. She seems to like it here, though." Jessa stretched.

"Who wouldn't like it here?" He chuckled and lifted her up from her spot.

"I wonder if Zeke has made his appearance yet," Jessa wondered aloud.

"Doubt it," Tristan said. Jessa and Tristan reached the shore at the same time. Jessa realized she was more exhausted this time than any other time. The waves were especially large for some reason. After she caught her breath, they continued towards the village. Tristan started to pick up his pace, and then broke out in a run towards his parents' house. Jessa was able to keep up rather well, but there was an uneasy feeling settling over her as she watched Tristan burst into the house.

"Mom! Where is Dad?" Tristan shouted.

Grace jumped from the intrusion. "He is with Royce practicing in the field. His next test is coming up soon and your father wants to make sure..."

Tristan was out the door before Grace was able to finish her sentence. Jessa quickly apologized for Tristan's behavior, and then ran after Tristan. He yelled back at her more than once to stay back with his mother, but she didn't listen. He was moving in the rainforest at a faster pace than she was used to. He started for a hill she hadn't seen before and trudging after him was difficult. She had very little energy left to continue up the hill, and she was about ready to actually turn around. It didn't help that there were obstacles and debris to run around. She couldn't believe how fast Tristan was going and that he was able to go so far without taking a break.

"Wait up, Tristan!" Jessa yelled when she realized how far ahead of her he had gotten.

He either didn't hear her or he didn't care because he didn't slow or turn around. Jessa tripped over a tree root and skinned her hands and knees. She looked up, and Tristan was nowhere to be found—not even a trace of a sound. She expected to at least hear a snap of a twig or leaves rustle, but it was as if he disappeared from the rainforest.

Jessa was wandering around on the hillside just above the rainforest line, heading in the direction she last saw Tristan. Time seemed to slip from her, but she didn't feel comfortable with how dark it was getting. She started calling out to him, yelling his name, hoping for a response. She figured it wouldn't take long for him to find her; he was her protector after all.

When the sun fell beyond the other side of the hill, she began to panic. He had disappeared a while ago and he still hadn't come back for her. She felt abandoned. There was nowhere for her to go—she didn't know her way back and there was no one around. The top of the hill was completely vacant. She squatted down on the ground and curled into herself. She didn't know what to do.

"I can do this. I can make it through the night on my own. I've done it before," Jessa coached herself.

She began to shiver as the night air picked up and blew across the hill. She missed her thick, hide blanket. The wind was getting stronger and stronger and threatened to push her over. After a while, she decided it was best if she moved to the rainforest tree line and try figure out how to get back to the village when it became light again. The howling night air was something out of a scary movie. It kept her on edge. Lightning flashed all around her and lit up the night sky. Her muscles were tense from her head to her feet.

Jessa thought that she would at least fall asleep at some point in the middle of the night, but that was not the as she watched light fill the sky. Bitterness rose up in her like bile; she could not believe that Tristan ran off and left her, knowing she was not familiar with the area. Her teeth chattered throughout the night and her muscles spasmed from the cold air. It rained at points during the night, and she had to huddle under a large leafed bush to try to keep dry.

By morning, she had run through several different scenarios in her head and nothing could explain what happened. Angry clouds loomed all around except for the top of the hill, which had clear, blue skies, the sun barely peeking through them. Jessa had never seen clouds do that before, and found it odd. It made her feel more alone than she had ever felt before. She shook her head at how quickly things had changed. One moment she and Tristan were on the beach and the next she was stranded in the middle of nowhere.

There was a comfort she was looking for, and it wasn't to be found. The tears that she had been fighting against were pulling at her eyes. She was tired of being the 'tough one.' There was no one around to see her break down. Even though it had only been one night, it felt like a lot longer. The fear she had felt throughout the night, she figured, had a lot to do with how long the night went.

Jessa was about to get up and find her way back down the hill when she heard her name ride on the wind. She looked around furiously. It was silent. She sprung up and began yelling back. She listened again. Nothing. She panicked and began running down the hill and yelling frantically. She was desperate to find who was out there and get back to the village—what she now considered home. Frustration boiled that it would take these circumstances for her to feel like the village was her home. No longer Minnesota.

"Jessa!" a voice called out. This time Jessa knew she couldn't be making it up. She responded immediately with her frantic cry for help. She was fighting back tears.

Grace came bounding down the hill.— She must have been on the other side. Jessa had no idea the wind carried Grace's voice that far,—; she also didn't care.— She ran towards the hill again, using what little strength she had to push forward as fast as she could. - She tried to hold back the tears, but amazingly after only one night of being alone she began to miss a familiar face.

There was a moment that she would never forget, the moment she was close enough she leaped into Graces arms and found a comfort there that she hadn't felt in a long time. She couldn't remember having that feeling since she was a little girl.

"You scared me to high heaven!" Grace shouted over the wind.

"I'm so sorry. I was following Tristan and he ran off without me!" she responded.

"Of course he did, silly," Grace said mysteriously.

"What do you mean 'of course he did'?!" Jessa asked.

"Come on; we need to get going before this wicked storm hits. Come on!" Grace urged.

They were going at a fast pace—not as fast as last night when she was running after Tristan, but fast enough. It felt as if they were running from something more than the weather. Jessa figured they must have really bad storms in this Land. Right now wasn't the time to ask questions, but she would be asking quite a few when they got back to the village.

Jessa started to recognize some landmarks. She was brought up to Lake Avery, her lake.

"Can you pack your things up fast?" Grace asked.

"Yes, but why?" Jessa responded.

"We don't have time for answers right now; I need you to hurry up and grab all your things. Hurry!" Grace shouted.

The urgency in her voice was what made her move quickly. Grace was not one to get this worked up over nothing. Jessa scaled the side of the rock and took the pathway through to her little cave and fumbled around, trying to find her pack with the glowing stones. She finally was able to feel around to the back of the cave and found it.

Soon she had the stones illuminating the dwelling. She didn't waste very much time; she was throwing things into her bag when she heard Grace shout to hurry up. Jessa growled, thinking to herself that she couldn't go any faster. She didn't know how she was going to bring the hide blanket. She yelled down to Grace, explaining that she would need help with the blanket. Grace told her to put it up high if possible and leave it behind. Jessa was so confused as to what could be happening. She finished packing her few things and went back down to where Grace was impatiently waiting.

"We have to hurry or we will never make it!" Grace said frantically.

"What is going on?" Jessa asked, but her question was lost on the raging sound of the wind.

They were running again; they came across a clearing and Jessa realized all too quickly that it was the village—or at least the remains of it. It looked as if everything had been torn down and put away, like a circus would do. She couldn't believe what she was seeing. Everything was gone. She looked around in horror, trying to figure out what was going on. She felt about as lost as she was when she first arrived at the Depot with her family. She missed her family.

"Where is Teagan?" Jessa asked.

"She is already safe. We are on our way to her and the others right now," Grace answered.

They continued to run in one direction, towards the caves Tristan brought her to with the glowing stones. Several times Grace warned her about not falling over the edge of the cliff. Eventually, they were hiking up a rocky terrain toward one of the other caves. Jessa got more cuts from falling onto sharp rocks. Grace actually had a few, too.

When they were in the cave, Grace navigated in the dark for a while and took Jessa's hand. After getting deeper in the cave, Grace took out a glowing rock. The rock illuminated a staircase made from the floor of the cave; it went down under the cave surface. Jessa looked down and it seemed to go forever. Grace didn't waste any more time. They descended the stairs at a whirlwind pace. Up above them, the wind was howling loud and sounded like it was gaining power. Her fear continued to grow.

The stairs ended and continued down a very narrow walkway, and if Jessa knew anything about directions it seemed as if they were walking right under the ocean floor. It was hot and sticky in the tunnel. Her clothes were drenched with sweat. She kept pace with Grace but was quickly losing energy. The craze of what had taken place in the last twelve hours or so and the lack of sleep were weighing in.

Grace could feel the change in pace and pulled her along. "We are almost there sweetheart; hang in there."

Jessa didn't want to push any further, but she understood there was a reason...even if she didn't know what it was. Eventually there was no need for the glowing stone because a light at the end was illuminating the pathway for them. There was an opening to a large cave with two sparkling ponds of ocean water, one was in the center and the other was off to the side of the cave. There were stalactite and stalagmites that were complementing the beautiful structure.

It was glorious, large space that everyone from Water Land was packed into. It was cozy and yet there was still space. It was as if the cave was in the middle of the ocean and the glittering ponds opened up into it but did not fill the cave. It was the oddest sight Jessa had ever seen, but she had heard about these places back on earth. There were also different plants that were spread out over the area, and small trees. Jessa thought it was impossible for that to occur, but it appeared they had used the light to help the plants grow. Several glow stones were around the area. It appeared the plants were contributing more oxygen in the cave. She was taking in the spacious area when she just about got knocked over by Teagan.

"I am so glad you are here! We were worried about you. Grace promised she would find you. Thank you, Grace!" Teagan turned to Grace.

"I'm glad you are safe. What are we doing here?" Jessa tried not to be overwhelmed by what was going on. Nothing made sense to her.

"Yes, come on; let's get you settled next to me. It sounds like we will be here for a while. The storm is only going to get worse." Teagan led the way to an area that was away from most of the crowds.

Jessa sat down and placed her pack next to her. She looked around seeing if she could find Tristan—she had a few things she needed to say to him. As she took a moment and watched people settle into a spot, she noticed that there weren't any males in the cave.

"Where are all the guys?" Jessa asked.

"They aren't coming," Teagan answered.

"What? Why?" Jessa asked.

"I don't know; ask Grace," Teagan answered.

It was a while before Grace wandered over with Omni, but in that time Jessa witnessed a close community take care of one another. It was a magnificent sight to see everyone do what they could to make others comfortable. Villagers had assumed the roles of head counting or food rationing and night watch, others helped with brain-storming games for the younger kids. Jessa watched all of this take place in a span of just a few hours.

"How are the two of you settling in? You comfortable under the circumstances?" Grace interrupted her thoughts.

"Considering the serious lack of information, I think we are okay," Jessa responded.

"I figured you would have some questions; that's why we are over here," Grace said as she found a comfortable spot to rest. The cave was getting a little warmer with all the movement taking place.

"What in the world is going on?" Jessa finally got the chance to ask.

"The men and boys have been summoned by Beneath Land royalty, otherwise they would be here to help and protect us. Unfortunately, the timing of this storm is making things extremely inconvenient," Grace began.

"Why would Beneath Land summon the men from Water Land?" Jessa asked.

"We have the best training in all the Lands; they need more protection because of a royal event taking place. There are others that come from other Lands to get training here, too," Grace said with pride.

"The weather is so different here," Teagan chimed in.

"This storm is not like anything we have seen on earth, nothing really compares to it, unless you combine all types of weather—hurricanes, tornadoes, and hail storms. It wipes off the entire island. But the most amazing thing happens when the storm is over: it all sprouts up right before your eyes, just the way it was," Grace said in wonder.

"How long will this last?" Jessa asked.

"Oh, dear...it can last a long time. Months, some-times. Again, time is measured differently here," Grace responded.

"*Months!*" Jessa and Teagan said in unison.

Chapter 22

She couldn't breathe. She was being choked by salt-water. Her mind was trying to grasp what was happening. Her eyes opened in a quick snap and she was staring out into a blur of water. Throat burning, arms flailing, bubbles rising from all around, and she wasn't able to move. Panic was beyond her as she tried to understand how she ended up in the middle of the ocean—once so inviting and calm, now a deadly threat to her existence. She opened her mouth to scream and saltwater filled her throat and burned all the way to her lungs.

"*Jessa*! Jessa, wake up!" Teagan shook Jessa's shoulders.

"What?" Jessa sat up, dripping in sweat. She looked around and it didn't take long to figure out she'd had a crazy nightmare.

"Clearly, you had a nightmare...care to share, since you woke up pretty much the entire place?" Teagan said.

Jessa shook her head. "I was drowning in my dream."

"That was some crazy drowning. But your nightmares have gotten fewer since we have been down here; maybe after another month they will be gone," Teagan stated, not knowing what else to say.

"It's already been a month!?" Jessa's voice cracked as she got the last word out.

"Well, something close to it. I've been trying to keep track, but it's not like these days are marked by hours or anything. Plus I can't see the sun. It really is just a guess," Teagan answered.

Jessa could not believe it had been around a month since she'd run through the rainforest with Grace and descended a long staircase to a cave. She felt suffocated and trapped in this space, no matter how large it was. She had dutifully done her assignments for that week that helped contribute to the new underground society of women. Jessa had been assigned laundry washing and Teagan would lay the clothes out to dry.

Jessa found herself wondering what Tristan was doing and if this separation would be good for them or the opposite. She remembered their last conversation— he'd said they should just be friends and wanted to know how to make her happy. The thought of him trying so hard brought tears to her eyes. Her days were filled with labor and the nights were filled with nightmares and restlessness. She could not get her body into a routine.

She didn't notice it at the time, but she had been sinking into a depression. She would have thought nothing of it if Grace hadn't pulled her aside one day to check on her. She had been in the middle of washing some clothing at one of the glittering ponds. Her hands were raw and chapped and her back ached from bending over the water. Several times, her clothes would end up wetter than the ones she was washing.

"Jessa, darling, are you doing alright?" Grace asked softly, her round frame coming into view in the periphery.

Jessa barely looked up. "I'm fine."

"It happens to all of us after a time down here. The rest of us have gotten used to it, so it takes a little longer," Grace offered.

"What happens?" Jessa looked at her questioningly.

"We all get a little down." Grace smiled gently.

Jessa shook her head. "I'm not down."

Grace raised her brows. "Okay."

"How often does this happen?" Jessa asked, staring at the water.

"Not very often; perhaps once a year," Grace answered.

Jessa just nodded, indicating she understood. Her motivation to continue conversation with Grace was low. She didn't have the energy to continue to ask questions. Grace sat next to her for a while in silence. The two of them seemed to be okay with not exchanging a word, until Grace got up to leave. She squeezed Jessa on the shoulder before she walked away.

Jessa would never catch up to the piles of clothes, but she was told she did not have to complete them all in one day. She would spend hours working on them, and once her body got too stiff to continue, she would take a break. Teagan had tried on more than one occasion to get her involved in an activity with her, but Jessa found no interest in them.

Jessa curled up on the bedroll, knowing she wouldn't

be able to fall asleep. She stared at a spot on the cave wall, the same spot she had been staring at for most of her time under the ocean. Her thoughts were quiet, her energy gone, and motivation evaporated. She curled even tighter into herself and drifted. She couldn't get her mind to stop.

"Jessa, wake up," Teagan said in a soft voice.

"What now?" Jessa was clearly struggling with the lack of sleep.

"Our assignments have changed," Teagan said.

"Oh?" Jessa didn't move from her spot.

"We have to go over to the lady that is handing out assignments; first ones get the better assignments," Teagan said.

"Ah." Jessa didn't care; Teagan hopped up and took off.

When she finally rolled out of bed, she walked over to a fresh water system that had been rigged up; it reminded her of Tristan's home. She could barely smile at the thought of him, and it didn't take long for her to realize that he was probably the one that construct-ed the very means for them to survive on fresh water in this cave. Her heart ached with a longing she had never felt before. She missed him. It had been too long since they last saw each other, and she couldn't help but wonder if he thought of her.

There were three people left in the line where the lady was handing out assignments. Jessa stopped behind the last person. She sighed, ran a hand through her hair, and looked around the cave. There were people talking and laughing. She narrowed her eyes at them, feeling jealousy wash over her, wishing she could be happy too. *I have to figure out how to make myself happy.* She recalled the words she had said to Tristan last they spoke.

"Do you think Zeke has gotten over his previous ma-te yet?" Teagan broke into Jessa's thoughts.

"Huh?" Jessa asked.

"Well, I was wondering if Tristan told you how long a person needs to mourn; because it would incredibly awesome if we got out of here soon and I was finally able to meet up with him," Teagan explained.

"Tristan didn't mention anything, other than to say everyone mourns. Hopefully you will be able to connect with him soon, though." Jessa tried to sound enthusiastic, but the conversation was not the least bit interesting to her.

"I got assigned to entertain the kids with games!" Teagan was excited.

"That's great," Jessa said.

"I wonder what you will get; you should have gotten here sooner."

Jessa shrugged and then moved up to talk to the lady. She did not show emotion when we was told she was part of the night watch. She would be going down the dark hall and sitting at the bottom of the stairs, watching for any changes or dangers. She was handed a sharp object; it wasn't sharp enough to be called a knife, but it looked very similar to what Jonah had been working on before she messed things up.

Jessa's eyes alighted on the object. That object saved her from losing her mind completely. She had found a new purpose: she was going to fashion that object into a weapon the same as Jonah had. Jessa didn't care about having to stay up all night—she wasn't sleeping well anyway. The object was light in her hand. With some work it would be thinner, shinier, and sharper.

Teagan looked disappointed when she overheard

Jessa's new assignment and couldn't keep from informing the lady she needed to switch roles with someone else. Jessa looked over at Teagan with a glint in her eyes and shook her head. Teagan, not having seen that look for a long time, backed down. Her assignment would be starting that very evening, so the lady recommended Jessa try to take a nap to help with the sleep change. Jessa ignored her and walked away.

Routine had long since settled over everyone in the cave. There was little time during the day to oneself; most of the time was spent preparing for the next phase of the day. Morning was marked by the reflection off the bottom of the ocean bed and into the cave, illuminating it with amazing blue colors. The evening was so dark that the glowing stones would only light up a small area; unless enough glow stones were used it would not be light enough.

Teagan seemed to fall gently into the routine, smiling and getting to know each of the people better. Jessa felt imprisoned in the cave, even amongst the glitter that danced on the ceiling and the pleasant people. The sense of community couldn't even shake her negative feelings. She wanted to be out in the open; she wanted to see Naoki. And Tristan. Her anger had worn off long ago when she realized it wasn't his fault she was left alone back on the hill.

The first night, Jessa was on edge. She watched the corridor and the long staircase. She would hear sounds throughout the night that would make her jump or flinch. When she started getting tired, she would practice using her weapon. She had been working on it earlier and was hoping to make a shiv. It was taking some time and effort, but she was finding motivation for this one thing, the only thing.

It was time to do some washing of the bedrolls in one of the pools. Jessa was glad that wasn't her duty anymore. She stared at the large water opening in the middle of the cave that opened to the ocean; she had just finished her night shift. As if in a trance, she walked slowly over to it. She had only her bag and the rope—both secured around her waist. She stared for a long time at the glittering water beneath her.

Teagan watched her sister from her bedroll, just getting up to take on the task of entertaining the kids. Teagan was hoping the end of the storm would come soon, so they could get out of the cave—but she tried to make the best of it. She would rather spend the time getting to know Zeke. If he were here, then she would be fine with being trapped in this place forever. It passed the time for her though. Lately all she could think about was Zeke; she wanted him to be over Julie. She was in the middle of daydreaming about it when she saw and heard a big splash. Her sister was no longer standing by the water hole—she had either fallen in or jumped.

Chapter 23

The water felt glorious. Jessa made sure to take a deep breath before she swam around under the water. She was trying to clear her ears as she continued her decent. She did not have a way to hold her breath for very long, but it was worth it. Jessa needed to get out of the cave. No more than a few seconds went by before she was nudged by a rubbery nose. *Naoki!* Jessa grabbed hold of Naoki and little time was wasted as she was brought to the ocean's surface, instead of being brought back to the opening into the cave.

"Naoki, have you been waiting for me?" Jessa asked as if Naoki was going to answer.

She barely got the words out of her mouth as violent

waves crashed over her. She was tossed more than once several yards away from Naoki. When Jessa looked towards the island, she could not see it through the wall of rain pounding down on her and all around. Thunder rolled above her and lightning lit the sky.

Naoki seemed agitated and was pushing for her to grab onto her again. Just before Jessa grabbed onto Naoki, she saw more than half a dozen black creatures rise up from the ocean, almost surrounding her. She was petrified and could not move. Naoki was doing everything she could to get Jessa to grab on. The creatures were nearing them at a quick pace. Jessa finally snapped out of it and grabbed onto Naoki. She was swift in getting Jessa back to the opening to the cave.

Jessa swam up through the opening coughing a little from swallowing some saltwater. Teagan helped her out of the hole, clearly worried. Teagan was wet as well and had told her that she had jumped in after her but could not find her. Jessa was shaking water out of her hair and breathing deeply. Jessa hoped Naoki was able to get out of the area safely. She worried about her.

"What the heck happened? Are you okay?" Teagan asked, unable to keep the worry from her voice.

"I had to get out of the caves," Jessa choked out.

"Was it worth it?" Teagan asked.

"It was horrific. Worse than anything my nightmares could conjure up. You wouldn't believe it, but there are at least half a dozen creatures out there. Plus the weather is so astronomically bad that the entire island appears to have disappeared!" Jessa yelped.

"You should not have done that."

"You are right," Jessa said.

"I hope the storm dies down soon," Teagan said softly.

"I have a bad feeling that it will be a while," Jessa said, recalling the destruction she witnessed.

"Miss Jessa," a little voice said.

Jessa tried to roll over and block it out because it was still night by her standards.

"Miss Jessa," the voice repeated.

"What?" she whispered in the dark.

"It's time to go."

Jessa sat upright and looked over to find Omni on the

edge of her bedroll. She didn't quite comprehend what she had said until she looked around and saw glowing stones illuminating the cave and people packing up their belongings. She wasted no time getting her things together and waking Teagan in the process. Teagan quickly followed suit.

Jessa couldn't help but smile the entire time they followed the long line of people leaving the cave the same way they had entered. She could almost skip, she was so excited. Teagan was unusually chatty. The trip up did not seem as long as going down into the caves; her excitement was giving energy to climb the many stairs.

"Are you nervous, Teagan?" Jessa inquired.

"I guess I am. What if he isn't over her yet? I just want him to want me without Julie getting in the way," Teagan answered.

"That makes sense. You think you will see him right away?" Jessa said as she struggled up the stairs. The energy she had at the bottom of the stairs was quickly fading, and it felt as if it was the hundredth step. It was hot and muggy going up the steps; it was starting to smell like sweat.

Jessa did not remember there being that many steps on the way down, and several times she had to take a quick break. Her legs were starting to protest the stairs and shake at each step. Teagan seemed to be struggling a bit as well; Grace was a few people ahead and Omni was holding her hand behind her. Omni was such a sweet girl. Jessa didn't recall spending very much time with her, though. Jessa couldn't recall very much of anything until she was working nights.

"Come on, Jessa; you of all people should be halfway running up these steps!" Teagan pushed.

Since there was another cave at the surface of the stairs, people did not have to put their glow stones away. Jessa was thankful to reach the top of the stairs and navigate with Teagan through the rest of the cave's pathways. It seemed the closer they got to light, the longer it took; Jessa knew it was because she was so excited.

"I am going to need to rest before going further," Teagan complained.

Finally she saw the people in front of her start to pack up their glow stones and slip into a light muted from how far she was behind in the line. She wished she were working the night shift when they discovered the storm had cleared so she could be at the front of the line. Eventually she put her glow stones in her satchel.

Teagan and Jessa stood at the top of steps and could not move, out of shock. A couple people behind pushed around them. The entire island was wiped away; all that was left was sand. Even some of caves were decimated into rubble. Jessa looked around as the wind whipped her hair around. She could see clear to the hill that she had been stranded on months before. It was miles away but there was nothing hiding it. There was no evidence of palm trees or any form of plant life.

"Should we be scared?" Teagan asked in horror.

"I'd say so; everything is gone. How do we live off of a land that isn't habitable anymore?" Jessa asked.

"Now seems like a good time to visit Mom and Dad," Teagan said.

Jessa just stared off toward the hill as she allowed her sister's words to get lost on the wind. She didn't feel like responding; she didn't feel much of anything, except numb. She could tell the moment when her internal switch went from caring to empty. There was too much to take in and she couldn't stuff anymore reasoning into what she was seeing.

All of the sudden she saw a group of people appear on the hill she was staring at. They looked like big ants as they trailed down the hill. Some of the women started running toward them, and some of them yelled out their mate's names. The ants on the hill must have been the men returning from the event they had to help with. The timing was, yet again, perfect.

"You're right; now is probably a good time to visit Mom and Dad," Jessa said, but as she turned to Teagan she saw she was standing alone. Teagan had taken off running toward the hill.

Jessa walked forward, wondering if she should run towards Tristan, wondering if he would care. The doubt kept her on that side of the island, far away from the hill. She gathered her strength and followed the ledge that lined the crashing ocean waves, working hard not to get too close to the edge. The cliff side was dangerous enough before the storm. The sun was high overhead, meaning it was the middle of the day. There was no evidence of the creatures that she saw, either. The wind was still strong, but not even close to the strength that it had before. She set some of her stuff down and was about to sit when she turned around and saw the happy union between the villagers. From her vantage point, it was just movement and cheers of joy traveling on the wind.

The moment the two groups collided in a glorious union of friends and family, they disappeared behind what Jessa would never be able to describe. The foliage and palm trees sprouted up instantly before her eyes, no damage to be seen—no mark of the storm. The very spot she was standing on filled with grass and plant life. This was what Grace had talked about: things going back to normal. Splendid colors filled her vision; she had to blink to maintain focus on the rapid change. It was magic. There was nothing else she could say to describe what happened.

The movement happened so fast she fell on her backside when the ground rebounded a little. She looked around and from what she could see, everything appeared to be just as it was before she left. The air was knocked out of Jessa. She rolled over to her side, coughing, trying to get air into her lungs. She should be shocked by what she had seen, but she wasn't. Her satchel fell to the ground and the contents spilled out.

"You must not be native," said a deep voice.

Jessa looked up and was instantly drawn to the light green eyes of a tall stranger. She did not recall seeing him in the village; she would remember seeing this particular person. He had jet-black hair, a smile that made her feel like he could read her mind, skin that had been exposed to some sun, and a body thick with muscles. She could feel herself being drawn in by more than just his looks, but something else.

"Where are you from?" the stranger asked.

She couldn't get the words to form; she knew something wasn't right and that she should feel fear, but she didn't know why. He extended his hand to her; she reached out and then snapped her hand back before they touched. *What am I thinking?* she thought. The stranger still held out his hand. She looked curiously up at him. She finally reached up, and when their hands connected she could feel an electricity flow between them. He helped her up.

"Got an answer yet?" he repeated.

Jessa ran her hand through her hair instinctively and stumbled through her answer. "You, ah, wouldn't know it."

"Try me," he responded.

"Minnesota," she said.

"Lots of lakes there, right?" he asked.

"Wh--who are you?" Jessa asked.

"I think you already know the answer to that," he said cryptically.

She tilted her head and narrowed her eyes, a long moment passed until she felt as if she got the air knocked out of her again.

"Cade," she whispered.

Chapter 24

Tristan felt it. The moment Jessa left the Land, he could feel a low buzz. Something wasn't right. He was hoping she would meet him on the hill with the rest of the females, but she didn't. He thought he saw her in the distance. But he knew—he knew she wasn't at Water Land anymore. His intention was to apologize and try harder to be her friend, help her to love this Land the way he did, once he got back from Beneath Land. *She must be really mad at me to punish me like this,* he thought. She knew he didn't want her to go to other Lands without him. This would be the best way to punish him for leaving without explanation. He caught up to his mother when she greeted Royce and his dad. He had hoped that Grace would have at least explained that he didn't have a choice.

"Mom, how did everything go with us gone?" Tristan asked, wanting to make sure everyone was taken care of in the caves.

"It went as well as anyone could expect in those circumstances. Where is Jessa?"

"Did you explain to Jessa what happened?" Tristan asked before answering.

"Of course, dear, I explained it as best as I could. She was right behind us on the way out of the tunnel." Grace turned around and pointed.

"She isn't here," Tristan said.

"Well, of course not; she is back there—we came running once we saw you. She may have stopped for a break," Grace reasoned.

"No, she is not here in Water Land anymore," Tristan answered.

"Don't joke about such things!" Grace yelled.

"I feel it, Mom; I know she isn't here," Tristan said.

Teagan came over to the family, looking a little frustrated. She couldn't find Zeke anywhere. She was hoping that she would get the opportunity to finally introduce herself. She hugged Royce and Jonah as the family gathered and noticed a change in the group. Concern was written all over Grace's face.

"Grace, what's wrong?" Teagan asked.

"Your sister left Water Land," Grace said through green tears.

"What? She wouldn't do that. She wouldn't just leave!" Teagan said, even though she didn't know if she believed that. Jessa had been acting strange in the caves; she wasn't sure what Jessa would do. Then she remembered what she had said just moments ago.

"Uh oh," Teagan backed up a few steps.

Grace and Tristan looked at her. "What?"

"I think she might have left to see Mom and Dad. I might have made a comment. I didn't mean it, but she might have meant what she said," Teagan said.

"I see," was all Tristan could say.

"I'm sure she will be back, but you are sure she is gone?" Teagan offered.

"I don't feel the pull anymore; she isn't here. I know exactly when she left." Tristan didn't believe she would be back.

Tristan walked away, not being able to hold it together in front of his family and Teagan any longer, and not wanting to make a fool of himself in front of them. Instead of going back to the place that he had called home for so long, he went to Lake Avery. He climbed the rock wall that wound its way to the path that led to Jessa's home.

When he reached the opening to the cave, he pulled out his glow stone and walked around inside. He saw the hide blanket sitting on a shelf. He knew it would have been too heavy to move to the underground safety location. His heart ached, squeezing it into a painful vise-like grip. Tristan was hoping for a different type of emotional reunion. He was hoping that maybe she missed him and would hug him, and then he figured she would probably yell at him for leaving her.

He had no reason to hide tears, because no one was around. It was quiet—painfully quiet. His legs gave out in the middle of the cave, and he let the pain roll over him in waves. He had to consciously tell himself to breathe, but he didn't care at the moment. Several hours later, it was the anger that forced him to his feet, out the doorway of the cave, through the pathways, and instead of climbing down the cliff, he jumped off the edge, plunging into the lake.

Teagan saw Tristan jump off the ledge into the water

and waited for him to surface. She figured he would be here rather than the village or his own home. When he surfaced, he just treaded water over by the waterfall.

Teagan called out, "Are you going to make me come out there?"

Tristan turned around to face her. "I'm sorry; I thought I was alone."

He swam over to the boulder she was sitting on and climbed out of the water. His body was covered in goose bumps. She gave him a look over and thought she never had a problem admiring a healthy body before. She needed answers.

"Are we going to meet up with her?" she asked.

"I don't know," Tristan answered.

"Perhaps you would like to meet our parents," she pushed.

"Maybe." He let his head fall forward and his dripping hair shadowed his eyes.

"Well, make a decision soon. I'm getting restless here; I need a distraction," Teagan said as she rose.

"You can't leave."

Teagan looked at Tristan, wondering why his voice sounded different. Tristan's head snapped up and as he was looking around, his eyes landed on a figure standing on the edge of the woods that surrounded the lake. Teagan followed his gaze and her eyes caught with another pair of eyes, belonging to the man she had been waiting for, for what seemed like a long time.

She wanted to run to him, to grab him and tell him how awful it had been waiting for him to come to his senses, but she stood there frozen, like an idiot. She didn't have the words to respond to his command. She sort of liked the sound of it; he wanted her to stay.

Tristan picked up on the need to give them alone time, since this was the first time they'd met. He pulled himself out of the water and walked off, drops of water trailing like bread crumbs to his next location. Goose bumps continued to cover his body, the windy air drying him but keeping him chilled at the same time. Pieces of hair fell in front of his face. He heaved a sigh, not knowing what to do next.

Teagan fidgeted with her shirt, uncomfortable under his gaze. He did not look away from her; he looked entranced. It made her feel giddy and nervous at the same time to be the cause for such attention. She swallowed and moved forward but stopped a few yards from him. She tried to read his body language but could not draw any conclusions.

"I suppose telling you what to do is the wrong way to start out," Zeke fumbled with his words.

"I don't mind," Teagan said, sounding more girly than she had in her life.

"My name is Zeke." He held out his hand as he tried to introduce himself.

"I'm Teagan. And I am your mate, right?" Teagan asked, her face getting red.

"Yes. You are." He blushed at how forward she was.

"You've been waiting for me for a long time, haven't you, Teagan?" Zeke asked.

"Yes, I have. A very long time," she responded.

About the Author

In *The Lands*, the first book published in her collection of writings, K. Newman has found the ability to utilize her passion of evoking emotion and bringing her audience to a place of caring for the members in the book. Her hope is to continue to bring the audience to a place of empathizing and understanding the struggles that each character goes through in this journey called life.

K. Newman has been writing since she was a teenager, in the form of poetry, and most recently found a strong passion for writing short stories and novels. K. Newman started this path with a dream that, she felt, had to be told. Her hope is to continue dreaming and creating a world where her audience can share in the adventure.

Connect With the Author

knewmanbooks@gmail.com
www.facebook.com/knewmanbooks

Be Watching for the Next Book of the Series:

THE GILE

Rivershore Books

jansina@rivershorebooks.com
www.rivershorebooks.com

www.facebook.com/rivershore.books
www.twitter.com/rivershorebooks
forum.rivershorebooks.com
blog.rivershorebooks.com

Made in the USA
Charleston, SC
28 January 2014